Extremities

Starscape Books by David Lubar

Novels
Flip
Hidden Talents
True Talents

Nathan Abercrombie, Accidental Zombie Series
My Rotten Life
Dead Guy Spy
Goop Soup
The Big Stink
Enter the Zombie

Story Collections
In the Land of the Lawn Weenies and Other Warped and Creepy Tales
Invasion of the Road Weenies and Other Warped and Creepy Tales
The Curse of the Campfire Weenies and Other Warped and Creepy Tales
The Battle of the Red Hot Pepper Weenies and Other Warped and Creepy Tales
Attack of the Vampire Weenies and Other Warped and Creepy Tales
Beware the Ninja Weenies and Other Warped and Creepy Tales

Extremities

Stories of Death, Murder, and Revenge

DAVID LUBAR

TOR® **TEEN**

A TOM DOHERTY ASSOCIATES BOOK

NEW YORK

EXTREMITIES

Grateful acknowledgment is made to the following publications, in which these stories originally appeared: "A Cart Full of Junk," "Running Out of Air," "Free Seas," and "Split Decision" in *Orson Scott Card's InterGalactic Medicine Show;* "Feelings" and "Morph" in *iPulpFiction;* "The Ex Box" in *READ Magazine;* and "Apparent Motives" in *Rush Hour.*

Interior illustrations by Jim Kay

Design by Greg Collins

A Tor Teen Book
Published by Tom Doherty Associates, LLC
175 Fifth Avenue
New York, NY 10010

www.tor-forge.com

Tor® is a registered trademark of Tom Doherty Associates, LLC.

ISBN 978-0-7653-3460-2 (hardcover)
ISBN 978-1-4668-1460-8 (e-book)

Tor Teen books may be purchased for educational, business, or promotional use. For information on bulk purchases, please contact Macmillan Corporate and Premium Sales Department at 1-800-221-7945 extension 5442 or write specialmarkets@macmillan.com.

First Edition: July 2013

Printed in the United States of America

0 9 8 7 6 5 4 3 2 1

For Mark and Alison

Contents

Author's Note

I am torn. (You will appreciate the delicious irony of those specific words as you make your way through this book.) Part of me feels that these stories need no introduction. I want you to plunge right into the worlds I've created and savor the darkness. Another part of me wants to tell you every detail about how this collection came into existence, and to explain the origin of every story.

By way of compromise, I'll say those things that seem most important. I'll say them briefly, and then step aside. First, this is not a book for children. Let us be clear about that. My other story collections, easily identified by the humanlike hot dogs on the covers, are perfectly fine for young folks. Those books are popular, and thus they are a hungry beast. I write lots of stories to fill that hunger. At rare and random times, without any plan on my part, a story will emerge that is too dark, too heartless, or, dare I say it, too evil, for my young readers. But the truth is, I love those stories. And I want to share them. So here they are.

There's really just one other thing I need to tell you. Some of these stories were written long ago. Thus, you will encounter such historical oddities as stores that rent movies on videotape, and people who live in a world without cell phones. I realize that this lack of technology might be more horrifying to some readers than scenes of death, murder, and revenge, but those sensitive souls will just have to deal with it. I thought about modernizing the older stories, but decided against this, because the setting is part of the fabric that creates the mood. I like the stories the way they are. I hope you do, too.

That's really all I have to say. I think I'll slither back into the darkness and commit a few more murders—on paper—while you're enjoying these. Sweet dreams . . .

Running Out of Air

Deeva sucked air and dug for the strength to hold her place in the middle of the pack. One more lap and it was over. For today, at least. *Stay in the middle and you won't get killed,* she thought, risking a glance over her shoulder, where the stragglers tailed out—one pair running slowly with awkward gaits, two more barely jogging, and one last girl desperately swinging her arms in a pathetic attempt to make her walk look like a run.

"Move it, you lazy cows!" Ms. Pelham screamed, cutting across the track toward the laggers. "This is supposed to be exercise." She grabbed the whistle that hung from her neck, and blew an ear-piercing blast.

"They should fire her," Kate Wilson muttered as she ran just ahead of Deeva.

They've tried, Deeva thought. She'd heard stories. They'd all heard stories. Each fall, the first thing every girl at Smithfield High did was check her schedule to see which gym teacher she'd been assigned. Deeva was zero for two, drawing Ms. Pelham last year, and again this year. Across the field, near the bleachers, Ms. Bright was teaching her class an Irish dance step.

It was almost comic. Or cosmic. Bright and Pelham. Heaven and hell. Good and evil. Ms. Bright smiled. She encouraged all the girls. She baked cookies. Ms. Pelham snarled. She yelled at every student, except for the few star athletes who could do no wrong. But she saved a special level of venom for the slackers—the fat, the weak, the uncoordinated, the sickly. If you couldn't run laps, Ms. Pelham would eat you up. Three times a week.

Deeva finished her last lap, then turned to watch the final scene of the drama.

"You're gonna fail!" Ms. Pelham screamed. She waved her stopwatch at the girls. "You miserable, lazy cows. You're not even trying."

The slow runners, Debby Muñez and Tonya Hark, stumbled in. Then the joggers, Amber Weiss and Tabitha Jordan, made it across the line. Behind them, the walking, gasping, red-faced mess of Betty Lozer staggered toward the finish.

"Run!" Ms. Pelham shouted. She glanced briefly away

to lash the rest of the class with her favorite phrase. "Keep your nose where it belongs."

Betty moved her lips, but Deeva was sure the girl didn't have the air for speech. Even so, she knew what Betty was trying to say. Asthma. One word. An explanation that any sane person would understand. Asthma.

But Deeva had seen Ms. Pelham dismiss all infirmities short of broken bones as nothing more than pathetic excuses. The invisible remained unacceptable. Asthma wouldn't stop a girl who really wanted to run. Deeva could imagine Ms. Pelham walking through a plague-struck village during the Dark Ages, screaming, *Get up! On your feet, you lazy fakers!* at the dying who littered the streets.

Deeva let out her own breath as Betty finished the lap. Her sense of injustice was tinged with relief. Betty took a lot of the heat, leaving less of Ms. Pelham's attention for the others. Deeva's relief was tinged with guilt. Someone should do something about this. But those words, *Keep your nose where it belongs,* hovered at the edge of her thoughts like a wasp.

The class filed inside as Ms. Pelham berated them for

their poor display of soccer skills. "We're going to keep drilling until you get it right," she told them. "We'll do it until you drop, if that's what it takes."

Deeva got her clothes from her locker. On the bench just across from her, she saw the four other laggers clustered around Betty. The girl was a sobbing, wet wreck now, sucking on her inhaler and drawing wheezy gasps of air.

"Get a doctor's note," Amber told her.

Betty nodded, then wiped her nose with her sleeve.

"You have to do something," Tabitha said.

"Friday," Betty said.

"You have an appointment?" Amber asked.

"Yeah."

"Hang in there," Tabitha said. "Just one more class. Then you're free."

The talk died for a moment as Ms. Pelham walked by, holding a sheet of paper and a roll of masking tape. A moment later, she passed by again in the other direction.

Deeva shoved her gym clothes in her bag. Through the glass window that separated the coaches' area from the locker room, she could see Ms. Pelham at her desk, eating grapes from a large plastic produce bag. She seemed to live on fruit, though Deeva was sure that when nobody was looking, Ms. Pelham gorged on burgers and fries.

On the way out of the locker room, Deeva passed the spot where Ms. Pelham had taped up the latest grades. The teacher was murder on grade-point averages. Next to slow runners, she seemed to hate good students the most. The smart, the ambitious, the college bound were at her mercy. The best and the brightest served only to fuel her rage. She rubbed in the damage with weekly grade postings, handwritten and secured to the wall with masking tape, a dangling display of low numbers laid out for all the world to see.

Deeva winced at the *83* next to her name. She knew she deserved better, but there wasn't much she could do about it. Ms. Pelham had branded her as a low 80s student, and that's where she'd stay, no matter how hard she tried or how well she played.

Betty walked over and leaned toward the sheet. She gasped, then said, "That's not fair."

It was worse than unfair, Deeva thought. Ms. Pelham had given Betty a 59. Failing. But tauntingly close to passing. Worse, the grade threatened to ruin Betty's summer with a makeup gym class.

The marking period ended on Friday. Even with a doctor's note for next marking period, there was nothing that could erase the F that Betty was about to get.

Deeva watched Betty walk over to the coaches' room. *Don't do it,* she thought as she drifted closer.

Betty opened the door. "What can I do to raise my grade?" she asked.

Ms. Pelham looked up from her snack and regarded Betty with contempt. "Try harder."

"I'm trying as hard as I can," Betty said.

"Then you'll fail."

Betty walked off and joined her waiting friends.

Deeva headed out, too. At least gym was over for the day. And at least she was passing.

They played soccer again on Wednesday, though a damp chill cut through the air. Deeva inhaled slowly. Fast breaths hurt her lungs. She noticed that Betty kept glancing at the track.

When Ms. Pelham blew the whistle and sent them to

do their laps, Betty asked the teacher, "How fast do I have to go to pass?"

Ms. Pelham told her.

As Betty fell behind the pack, her four friends stayed with her, encouraging her.

Deeva dropped back toward the rear of the main group. It was safe. She knew Ms. Pelham wouldn't be watching her today.

Betty's gasps grew louder as she struggled to run.

Deeva clenched her teeth, wishing there were some way she could lend strength to Betty. Or sanity. *Just stop,* she thought. There weren't any degrees of failure here. A 50 was no worse than a 59. Even a zero was no worse.

As Betty ran, Ms. Pelham kept waving her stopwatch. "You're way behind," she said. "If you don't hurry, you'll never make it."

Deeva winced as Betty put on a burst of speed. It lasted for only a couple of steps. Betty stumbled and fell to the cinders. She pushed herself to her feet, took two more steps, then fell again.

She lay on the track, her chest heaving, one cheek pressed to the ground, her mouth open like a dying fish.

Ms. Pelham walked away. Betty's friends rushed over to her.

"She can't breathe!" Amber yelled.

Ms. Pelham shook her head in disgust. "Nikki," she called to her favorite pupil, "go get the nurse."

Nikki ran toward the school. Ms. Pelham walked back to Betty and stared down. Her expression showed nothing but annoyance. "Finish your laps!" she screamed at Betty's friends. "You've already lost points. Last one in gets an F."

The girls dashed off.

Deeva finished running, then huddled with the others, watching as the nurse came. And then the ambulance.

The story spread rapidly, growing and changing, mutating the way all school events do. But two points remained relatively unaltered: Betty was in bad shape. And Ms. Pelham wasn't in trouble. She'd told the administration that she did everything she could to keep Betty from overexerting herself, but the girl just wouldn't listen.

The next day, Deeva stayed late to audition for the school play. At one point, as she waited her turn, she saw four figures pass by in the hallway. Betty's friends.

There was something about the way they walked that

caught her attention. After Deeva read her lines, she left the auditorium and headed toward the gym.

As she reached the end of the corridor, she heard voices coming from the locker room. She slipped the door open and moved inside, ducking down and staying close to the lockers. Ahead, she saw five clustered figures—Debby, Tonya, Amber, and Tabitha. At the center was Ms. Pelham.

Her posture seemed odd. It took Deeva a moment to realize why. Ms. Pelham's hands were behind her back. In the light spilling from the coaches' room, Deeva saw that the gym teacher's wrists had been bound with masking tape. The office showed signs of a brief struggle. The teacher's chair was turned over. Her desk lamp was on its side. An apple and a handful of grapes were spilled across the desk. A couple of stray grapes had fallen to the floor.

"You girls are in big trouble," Ms. Pelham said.

"Hey, we can lie just as good as you," Tonya told her. "Nobody knows we're here."

"It's our word against yours," Amber said, tossing the roll of masking tape up in the air and catching it. "Nobody would believe nice girls like us would do anything bad. And we wouldn't. Not normally. But you're a special case."

The girls seemed to be waiting for something. Deeva sat and made herself comfortable. Time passed. She heard faint sounds through the wall as the boys came in from football practice, followed by more noise as they left the building. Soon after that, Debby slipped out and went to the back door, opened it briefly, then returned to the coaches' room. "It's clear. Come on. Let's go." She gave Ms. Pelham a push.

Deeva crept outside, keeping far enough back so they wouldn't spot her. The girls took Ms. Pelham to the track.

"It's very simple," Debby said. "We're going to run a race. Just one lap. You win, we cut off the tape."

Ms. Pelham laughed. "A race? Against you girls? It doesn't matter if my hands are tied. I'm an athlete. A real athlete. Not like you girls, who can't even—"

"On your marks," Amber said.

The other three girls turned to face forward on the track.

Ms. Pelham shook her head. "You are in so much trouble." A smile crossed her lips, as if she was already planning her revenge, or perhaps relishing her coming victory on the track.

"Get set," Amber said.

The girls crouched in poor imitation of sprinters.

"When this is over, you're all going to suffer," Ms. Pelham said. She leaned at the waist and put one foot forward. "But first, I'm going to make you eat dust. Stupid cows."

"Wait. I almost forgot." Amber stuck her hand in her pocket. Deeva heard a crinkling sound. Then Amber reached toward Ms. Pelham and slipped something over her head.

Deeva smothered a gasp as she watched Amber strip a length of masking tape from the roll and fasten the plastic produce bag around Ms. Pelham's neck.

"Go," Amber said.

The other three girls jogged off.

Ms. Pelham froze from the neck down. Her head swiveling rapidly from Amber to the runners, who were already widening their lead.

"Go," Amber said again, as if speaking very patiently to someone who wasn't bright at all.

Deeva saw the bag puff out as Ms. Pelham exhaled, then cling to her face as she drew a panicked breath. The clear plastic, fogged with moisture now, flattened on either side of her nose.

Deeva opened her mouth. One shout would put a stop to this. As she looked at the figures on the track, scenes from the past flooded her mind, along with a phrase she'd heard shouted far too often. *Keep your nose where it belongs,* Deeva thought.

Taking a slow, deep breath of the cold night air, Deeva turned and walked back to the locker room. Behind her, the crunch of feet on cinders faded, like the tail end of a dying gasp.

Split Decision

So, New York or Chicago?"

"I don't know," Greg said. "I think you're crazy going to either place. You can't run away."

"Sure I can," I said. "All my dad cares about is that stupid woman he married. I can't believe she's going to have a baby. I'm out of here. The only question is—New York or Chicago?"

"Ask Spooky Sheila," Greg said.

"No way. She creeps me out." I glanced at the back of the room toward Sheila Delphini's desk. She was playing with her hair, braiding and unbraiding several strands, and paying no attention to the teacher. Not that I was paying any attention, either. Why take notes when you aren't planning to stick around?

"But she'll tell you what will happen," Greg said. "I've heard she's got some kind of way to see the future."

I'd heard the same rumors. Kids had whispered stories about Sheila for years. I wasn't sure whether I wanted to believe any of that stuff. But it couldn't hurt to see what she thought about my problem. When the bell rang at the end of the period, I walked over to her desk.

"I've got a question," I said.

She raised her eyes up toward me without lifting her head. Her irises were so light blue, they almost seemed clear. A chill ran through my body and along my arms.

"You're going to split," she said.

"How'd you know?"

She didn't answer. Maybe she'd heard me talking to Greg. I'd have to be more careful. If my dad found out, he'd murder me.

"Should I go to New York or Chicago?"

She reached out and grabbed my hand. Then she closed her eyes. She took a long, slow breath. I waited. She breathed. Behind me, I heard people shuffle in for the next class. Just as I was about to pull my hand away, her body jerked like she'd been slashed across the back with a whip. Her fingers dug into my palm. She opened her eyes but didn't say anything.

"Tell me."

She released my hand. "The future can hurt."

"I don't care. Tell me."

"New York if she has a boy. Chicago if she has a girl."

It took me a moment to realize what she was talking

about. "My dad's wife?" I couldn't bring myself to call her my stepmother.

Sheila nodded. A single tear trickled from her left eye. She was starting to creep me out.

"But I don't want to wait. . . ."

She shrugged. I fled. Something about her made my stomach feel like I'd swallowed razor blades dipped in acid.

I caught up with Greg in the hall and told him what she'd said. "Crazy, huh?" I asked.

"Maybe. But have you gotten any better advice?"

"Nope."

"Then wait. See what pops out."

"No way."

I wasn't going to wait. I had to get out of there. But I needed to make sure I didn't get caught. My chance came sooner than I'd expected. Saturday, late in the afternoon, Dad's wife went into labor. She was three weeks early. It was my perfect opportunity to split. They probably wouldn't even notice I was gone until tomorrow. The moment they left for the hospital, I crammed clothes into a duffel bag and headed for Sawtooth Ridge. Lots of trains went through there. I could hop one for New York or Chicago. I just needed to know which way to go.

I pulled out my cell phone and called Greg. "I need a huge favor. Go to the hospital—okay? Wait at the place where they put the new babies. You know where I mean?"

"Yeah. I know. Are you really doing this?"

"I am. So help me out, okay?"

"All right. I'll call when I have news."

I hung up and went over to the tracks. The ridge was on a steep grade, so the trains slowed down a lot as they came through. I'd read books where people hopped trains. It didn't sound hard, as long as you were careful. I wasn't worried about getting hurt. Sheila said I'd go to New York or Chicago, so obviously I was going to survive the trip.

It was getting dark. There were no lights anywhere near the ridge. I didn't like the idea of hopping a train when I couldn't see what was going on. I called Greg again, but there was no answer. I figured I couldn't count on him.

"Forget the stupid prediction," I said. I decided I'd take the next train that came along.

About ten minutes later, an eastbound train came

crawling up the ridge. "New York," I said. That would be fine. I waited until the engine and the first couple of cars passed, then started jogging along. I had to be careful—the tracks were close together.

I saw a boxcar with a sliding door. I grabbed the handle and pulled myself toward it.

As I was dangling from the outside of the boxcar, my phone rang. It was stupid to try to answer it, but habits are hard to break. When phones ring, we grab them. I fumbled with one hand, got my phone out of my pocket, and flipped it open.

"Twins," Greg said.

"What?"

"A boy and a girl."

The words entered my brain and sat there like a foreign phrase. They didn't seem to tell me what I needed to know. Before I could say anything to Greg, the train rocked as it entered a sharp curve at the bottom of the ridge. The phone slipped from my fingers. I leaned over to try to catch it, and lost my balance. As I started to fall, I panicked and hooked an arm through the boxcar door handle. My duffel bag, which I'd looped over my neck, swung out from my other shoulder.

The phone clattered to the ground. I didn't care. Something else had my attention. Ahead, far too close, I saw a westbound train headed right for me. I tried to swing the duffel bag out of the way, but I couldn't get any leverage.

As the other train reached me, I heard Sheila's words.

"New York if she has a boy. Chicago if she has a girl."

She'd had both. I felt a jolting pain when the duffel bag got snagged by the passing train. I tried to yank my arm free, but it was wedged in the door handle.

Sheila was right. I was going to New York and Chicago. As pain beyond anything I'd ever known ripped through my body, I remembered her first words.

"You're going to split."

Right.

Apparent Motives

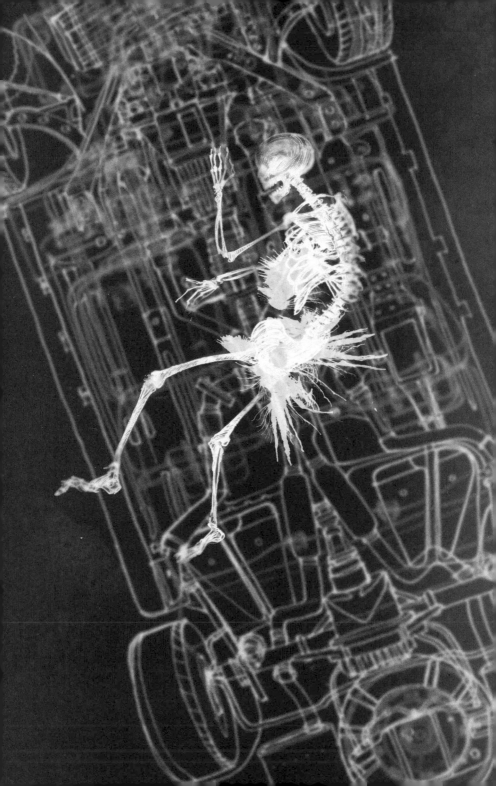

slunk into first period, my head down and my shoulders drooping as if someone had severed the muscles across my upper back. All the way to my desk, I felt the eyes checking me out. The air rippled with whispers. I sighed and sat, wondering who would be the first to intrude.

"Hey, what's up?" Dylan Kean asked, leaning over from his seat on my left.

"Nothing." I rested my chin on my hands and waited for the class to start. I tried not to sigh too often during the rest of the period.

After class, Dylan dogged me on the way out to the hall. "Come on, Stan. You look awful. Share the pain. What's up?"

I turned to face him. "Can you keep this to yourself?" Dylan wasn't known for his discretion. But I didn't have any close friends in school, and I needed to tell someone. It might as well be him.

He nodded. "You bet."

"My dad's splitting," I said.

"No kidding?" Dylan's eyebrows rose and a brief

half smile danced across his lips. I watched as he pulled his face into a mask of sympathy and concern. "That's awful."

"Yeah. It's weird, too. He's trying to hide everything, but I found all this stuff."

"Like what?"

"Like he's quitting his job. My PC was down, so I was using his to write a paper. You know how the file menu lists the last couple of documents that were opened?"

Dylan nodded again. "Sure."

"There it was—a resignation letter. He didn't even plan to give them two weeks' notice." I shook my head. "That job was his life. Now he's walking away from it."

"Hey, that doesn't mean anything," Dylan said. "My dad changed jobs last year. I could name a bunch of kids in our class whose folks changed jobs." He started to mention some examples, but I cut him off.

"Did any of them buy a rail pass?" I asked. "I found the receipt in his desk drawer—he can ride the train anywhere he wants for sixty days."

"People take vacations," Dylan said.

"Do they bookmark websites about quick divorces or download stuff about abandonment laws? That's

probably the reason he didn't split months ago—I just
turned eighteen last week. If he'd left when I was a mi-
nor, the cops could go after him for support payments."
I listed the rest of the evidence: a newspaper article on
the best places to live in Mexico, another article about
Canada, ads for apartments in several cities, tons of
other stuff. The conclusion was undeniable. "I mean, that
must be why he's going by train. The cars are in both
their names, and he doesn't want to take any chances."

"That sucks," Dylan said. "Does your mom know?"

"I doubt it. I'm not sure what would be worse—if she
found out now, or if she found out after he disappeared.
What do you think?"

The late bell rang before Dylan could give me his
opinion. "Hey, thanks for listening," I said. "I'm kind of
glad I told someone." I hurried down the hall to my next
class, struggling to keep the sad expression on my face.
It was tough. I really wanted to smile. But that would
screw up everything.

Damn, this was working out perfectly. By the end of
the day, it was obvious Dylan had broadcast the news
to every ear he could borrow. Glances, whispers, and
small acts of kindness were scattered across my path.

A girl who'd never looked at me before gave me a sad smile in the hallway after third period. My chemistry teacher cut me some slack when I botched an experiment. Two people offered me a space at their table during lunch. The school knew.

Excellent. My bad fortune would spread like a virus, carried home by all those Dylan had infected. Once enough people accept a rumor, it becomes a truth. I'd give the process another day, just to make sure the story permeated far and deep enough to become real. The word was out—my dad was leaving my mom.

I watched him at dinner that evening, right after he got home from that job he pretended to love. He grunted when she put his food in front of him, then started eating without waiting for her to sit.

He took a bite of the string beans, then glared at her. "These aren't cooked enough."

She reached for his plate. "I'm sorry."

"Leave it!" He grabbed a knife and sawed at his steak. "Why the hell did you buy this? It's tough. Don't you even know how to pick a decent cut of meat?"

"I can make something else."

"Just shut up and let me eat," he said. "Whatever else you make won't be any better."

I clenched my teeth and kept silent. I knew that if I went to her defense, he'd only make her suffer more later. I'd learned that the hard way. At least he pretty much ignored me, except when we were in public and he was playing the role of Super Dad. I'd happily trade places with her if I could, taking whatever he lashed out with if it meant she'd be spared. But I guess my heart wasn't the one he needed to crush.

By the end of the meal, he'd found a dozen more faults. Little things. Small digs. But unending. The death of a thousand cuts. He disapproved of everything she did. Her friends. Her interests. Her enjoyment of life. I kept waiting for her to decide she'd suffered enough. I'd waited eighteen years, hoping she'd find the courage to leave the bastard. But nothing pushed her over the edge. She took it all.

She'd never leave him. I'd asked. I'd suggested and I'd begged. But she'd been raised to believe that marriage was for life. We argued so fiercely at times that I wanted to grab her and shake her. "Things aren't so bad," she'd say, her voice betraying the truth that things were awful. "I took a vow. Till death do us part."

He'd never leave her, either. Their relationship was too convenient. She cooked and cleaned and absorbed his abuse with just the right amount of suffering to feed his sick needs. For every ounce of crap he swallowed at work, he came home and dumped a bucketful on her.

The worst part was how he hid that face from the world. Outside the house, he was Mr. Cheerful. The perfect family man. Hard worker. Friend to all. Great guy. Everyone's pal. First to buy a round of drinks, and last to leave a party. A real charmer.

Since neither of them would end the marriage, it was up to me to get rid of him. Then Mom could finally have the life she deserved. But I knew that if he just disappeared, the police would search until they found an answer. There was no way I could defeat forensic science. I wasn't arrogant enough to think I was smarter than the lab guys. So I decided to circumvent the problem. The hunt for fibers and DNA wouldn't even begin. He'd vanish—but not without a trace. When the police uncovered a trail leading elsewhere, they'd nod knowingly and write it off as another man in search of a better deal. *Sorry, ma'am, there's not much we can do. He could be anywhere. Might even have left the country. You could file a missing person report, but to be honest, it's probably not going to do much good.*

He'd be gone, and we'd be fine. Mom had a degree in accounting. She wanted to work, but Dad refused to let her get a job. We'd be okay for the short term, too. Dad may have been a bastard, stuck in a job he hated, but he was a hell of a breadwinner. He never let Mom forget that he earned every penny that came into the house. Tomorrow night, he'd get something else he'd been earning for a long time. He was restoring an old Camaro in the garage. That was his hobby. It kept him out of the house, but not so far away that he couldn't shout for Mom if he wanted something. Long ago, I'd thought about kicking out the jack when he was underneath the car. But that was no good. The jack wasn't the kind that slipped easily. The base was large and solid. It would be too suspicious an accident.

But the garage itself was perfect for my plan. There was a tarp on the floor. I'd already selected the hammer. I'd wipe it clean just in case and leave it in the tarp when I wrapped him up. I knew where to take the body. Miller

Road ran right along the south side of the landfill. Parts of the old fence had fallen down. If I put him in the right spot, he'd be bulldozed under a ton of garbage by the end of the day. He'd never be found. Of course, no one would bother looking. What would be the point? He'd obviously run off. Even the most inept detective would uncover some of the clues I'd planted. As for Dad—he wouldn't notice anything. He rarely used his computer, even before he got wrapped up with that car. It reminded him too much of work. There was no reason for him to look at the bottom of the stack of papers in his lower left desk drawer or in a shoe box in the back of the closet. No reason for him to find anything.

Last month, when the plan had first flared through my mind, I wasn't sure I could actually kill him. But each evening, my resolve strengthened as I watched him beat Mom down with words. Every angry jab he spoke was a nail in his own coffin. Not that there would ever be a coffin.

School was challenging the next day. I was eager to finish the plan I'd set in motion. But I also had to maintain the mood of despair. It helped to think about Mom's old photo album. She'd been a different person before they

were married. Happy. Fun loving. She'd gone water-skiing
and rock climbing. She'd sung in a chorus in high school
and spent one summer bicycling through Italy. She'd
even seemed happy in the early photos of them together.
But each turn of the page revealed less joy. The photos
grew more posed and rigid. Her smile and the glow in
her eyes gave way to the grim face of a prisoner serving
a life sentence.

"You doing okay?" Dylan asked when I took my seat.

"Surviving," I said. I could tell he was hoping for another gem to share with the world. But he'd already
served his purpose.

The girl who'd smiled at me yesterday talked to me
today. She even put her hand on my shoulder for a brief
moment. There were definitely benefits to being the
victim of a heartless parent.

That evening, after dinner, I followed Mom into the
kitchen. "You all right?" I asked.

She glanced at me, her real despair far deeper than
the mask I'd worn at school. "I'm fine." It was barely a
whisper.

Maybe he'd finally pushed her too far. He'd been nas-
tier than ever at dinner, and she'd been even quieter,

almost as if she'd made a decision. Though that was probably just wishful thinking on my part. If she left him, I'd be spared from having to commit murder. But I didn't want that reprieve. Now that I'd made up my mind, I couldn't bear the thought of him living. I waited for her to say something more, but she just shuddered and started scraping the plates. My plan wouldn't be altered.

I took a long walk. My nerves were on edge, but only because I was finally close to my goal. It would be over soon. He'd be gone. Mom would be free. She'd be happy for the first time in ages. We'd be happy. When I'd waited long enough so I was sure he'd be in the garage, I headed back home.

I got to the house about the same time as the police.

Mom stopped me out front, at the bottom of the porch steps. "There's been an accident." Her face seemed deathly pale, even in the reflected wash of the amber and red emergency lights.

"What happened?"

"Your father was working on that car. The jack slipped. . . ."

I felt the universe take a sharp twist, throwing everything out of sequence. "Is he all right?"

She opened her mouth to speak, then squeezed her eyes shut and buried her face in my chest.

I stayed by the porch, comforting her, letting the sense of relief sink in. It was over. And I hadn't had to kill him. I'd been spared, after all. Not that I couldn't have done it. I was willing to do it for her. But it was so much better this way.

"Ma'am," a polite voice said.

I glanced toward the door. A policeman was standing on the porch, studying Mom.

"Yes?" she asked, moving to join him.

"Just a couple of questions." He held up a receipt for the rail pass. "Did you know about this?" I could see other papers in his hand. Pieces of the trail I'd created.

"No," Mom said. She froze halfway up the steps. "I've never seen it before. What is it?"

Oh, God. I could hear it in her voice. Mom was a terrible liar.

The policeman could hear it, too, I guess. "I think you might want to contact a lawyer," he said.

As the policeman went back inside, I walked toward Mom. She scurried away and thrust a hand out, as if to hold me off. As if to protect me from herself.

"You didn't do anything wrong," I said.

She shook her head. "I did everything wrong."

The truth caught in my throat. It wouldn't set her free. It would just add to her misery.

One policeman stood by the sidewalk, watching us. All the other cops had gone inside. To look for more evidence, I guess. They'd find it. I'd made sure of that. There was a ton. Enough for anyone to discover, I realized. Even someone who hadn't been looking.

Feelings

D oesn't it feel like it's sucking you right in?" Don had to shout over the rumble of the westbound trucks that shot past us at speeds well above the limit.

"Yeah!" I shouted back. Even twenty feet away, the wind and force of those big semis were something to feel. I'd forgotten how powerful they were. I hadn't taken the shortcut to the mall in ages. It was mostly used by kids who weren't old enough to drive. Ever since Don had started dating Jennie, we really hadn't done much of anything together. Maybe I was trying to recapture some of the old times by going this way instead of taking the car.

"Gets the blood pumping," Don said. He stopped walking and turned toward the chain-link fence that ran along the top of the ridge.

I had no idea what he meant. Trucks and noise didn't do anything for my blood. But I stopped, too. Another truck shot past, blowing my hair, catching at my shirt. Between the trucks, packs of cars and vans weaved across six lanes of black asphalt—three lanes eastbound, three westbound, with a low divider in the middle.

"Hard to believe all those people have somewhere they need to go," I said. It wasn't rush hour yet, but that didn't matter on this stretch. The road was always busy.

"There's a pattern," Don said. He stepped closer to the fence. "See it?"

I watched the traffic for a minute. "Nope. I just see a lot of people going east, and a lot of others going west. What kind of pattern?"

Don didn't answer.

Instead, he climbed the fence and hopped down on the other side.

"Where're you going?" That was a strange thing for him to do. But I wasn't worried. Don was the most cautious person on the planet. He even washed his fruit. He buckled his seat belt when he was moving his car from the driveway to the garage. He was Mr. Careful.

"Right across, man. I'm going right across. It's all in the timing." His voice sounded flat and far away. Another truck blew by, drowning Don's next words.

"Stop kidding around." A ripple of worry flashed through my guts. "Come on. Let's get going." I moved closer to the fence. But it was silly to worry. Whatever Don was doing, I knew he wouldn't go down the hill and step onto that highway. I would have bet anything on that.

I would have lost.

"Here I go!" Don screamed. He let out a whoop and took off.

"No!" I grabbed the fence, frozen. Beneath my fingers, the metal vibrated from the rumble of the traffic.

Below, Don was crossing the interstate. I had no idea why he was doing it. He ran straight for the other side, speeding up or slowing down a bit as he went, lane by lane, across one of the busiest strips of road in the state. It was almost like some damned video game. Horns blared all over the place. The scream of tires tore through the air as drivers slammed on their brakes, though there wasn't a prayer that any of them could stop that quickly. A white Taurus nearly ran off the shoulder as it swerved around Don. A red Camaro, the driver holding a phone to his ear, blew past Don, inches from his back, never slowing.

Don hurdled the center barrier without pausing, just getting out of the way of a black Nissan wagon. His shirt rippled from the wind as the wagon passed him. There was nothing in the fast lane. He jogged through the middle lane seconds after a Mustang shot by, tires squealing, leaving twin tracks of rubber on the road. Don reached the slow lane, still looking straight ahead.

He nearly made it.

Maybe, just maybe, he would have been okay if it had been a car that ended his run. A car might have cost him just a few months in a cast if the driver had braked hard enough and fast enough. Maybe. But it was a truck that hit Don. I suspect the driver didn't even feel the jolt. Don sure as hell felt the jolt. Standing on the other side, clutching the fence, even I could feel the jolt.

Jennie looked lovely at Don's funeral. God forgive me— that's what I kept noticing. There I was, hearing a minister explain how this was all for the best and beyond anything we could understand. There I was, trying not to look at a box that held the crushed remains of my best friend. Don was gone, I didn't want to be there, and Jennie looked lovely.

Jennie was near the front, across the aisle and several rows ahead of me. She was wearing a simple dress that draped her body and clung to it in ways that made me want to reach out and run my hand against the fabric.

I forced myself to look away from her. Don was dead. I still couldn't believe that my best buddy had lost a game of tag with a truck right in front of my eyes.

A flicker of motion drew my attention. Jennie had tossed her head slightly, throwing her black hair from her shoulders. In the sunshine streaming through the church windows, her hair seemed both to gleam and to swallow the light. It was a hypnotic mix, absorbing and reflecting the beams in ways that made my mouth grow dry. It was almost as if sunlight existed only so Jennie could bathe in it.

Around me, everyone was rising to sing a hymn. The church was filled with adults and with Don's friends from school. The air was thick with the scent of too many flowers. We all lifted our voices and sang about crossing one last river. Maybe that was a poor choice of hymns, but nobody seemed to notice. I sneaked another glance at Jennie, watching her throat move as she joined in. Her neck was smooth and soft. There were too many voices for me to pick hers out, but I suspected it was like honey and stardust.

I looked at the coffin. My mind knit a scene where the polished wooden box suddenly flew open. Don, badly put back together by an undertaker who knew it would be a closed-casket service, sat up and said, "One more chance. I know I can make it. And this time, you're coming with me, pal." He pointed at me, one finger extending from the mush that had been his hand. Then he put the hand on the edge of the coffin and stepped out.

I shook my head, physically trying to fling the image from my mind. It flew off, but I knew others would come to fill the space. I knew all too well that my mind would never run dry of horrors.

We sat and bowed our heads in prayer. As the words slipped from my lips, memories of Don glided through my mind. He was always so cautious. When we went through town, he'd cross the street rather than walk past the wrong gang. He'd checked the air pressure in his tires more often than anyone on the planet. Now he was dead. But I envied his life. Quiet, careful Don had been dating Jennie. They went out for two months, almost from the time Jennie had come to our school.

Head still bowed, I opened my eyes a slit and looked in her direction. I wondered if she'd ever worn that dress on a date with Don. What would it be like to touch those shoulders? How would it feel to hold her hand?

I envied him, and I felt awful about it. That was the last thing I needed. I already felt awful about the funeral. I'd almost stayed home. At the first sight of the coffin, it took all my strength not to turn and run from the church. The funeral gave my mind too much to play with. And there was worse ahead. Far worse. I knew it was crazy. What kind of person is scared of a graveyard in the middle of the day?

My kind, I guess.

That's my dark secret. I don't know how or why I'd gotten this way. If I look back at my childhood, I can remember things and people and events, but I can't recall feelings—not with any clarity. Somewhere along the line, I picked up a lot of fear. I didn't like it. But I couldn't help it. Stories I'd read or movies I'd seen stayed in my mind. Scenes of the dead rising terrified me, scenes of familiar people turning into monsters haunted me. Whenever I was alone with a friend at night, I'd almost see him shift and change into something hungry for my flesh. Walking down a dark street, I could hear the creatures stalking me. I avoided mirrors and basements.

The tales of Poe, tales of being buried alive, entered my mind at the oddest moments. I'd imagine the school collapsing on me, burying me in rubble, leaving me scratching weakly at my prison, unheard by the rescuers who passed inches from my dying body. I'd feel my heart speed up when I went past the construction site on the south side of town, imagining a thousand ways I might slip into the pit and be suffocated by an avalanche of dirt. Buried forever beneath the new supermarket.

The prayer ended. We raised our heads. The minister spoke more words. We rose and filed out. I watched Jennie. She walked up to Nick Ferrano, the class clown. Nick was behaving himself—no jokes today. I would have ripped his heart out myself if he'd tried to be funny. But he was as torn up as the rest of us.

Jennie said something to Nick. He said something to her. She put her hand on his arm for a moment, just the lightest touch, almost like someone reaching for a box of cookies in a store but not yet sure if it was the one she wanted. Another twinge of envy flashed through me as I turned away from them and left the church.

Don's parents were outside, looking lost. I didn't know what to say. I imagine nobody knew what to say. We filed past and shook their hands, and most of the girls cried, and most of the guys cried but tried to pretend that they didn't.

It was awful.

After I reached the parking lot, I watched Jennie walk to her car. She looked just as good from the back. The black fabric swirled around her calves, weaving a spell over me. She was giving Nick a ride.

I went to my own car and pulled in line with the rest of the people. The cemetery wasn't far. After I parked and turned off the engine, I sat where I was, staring at the rows of headstones and wishing I'd never stumbled across late-night commercials for all those low-budget zombie movies. My mind filled with scenes of hands pushing through the ground, bursting free of the graves. I wondered if I could slip away, or slink down in the seat until the funeral was over.

Nobody seemed to notice me. I sat, building up the nerve to watch them put the coffin in the ground. Jennie and Nick walked up the path to the grave site. Even from a distance, she stood out, a vision painfully lovely in this cold field of death.

The graveside ceremony started.

I watched from the car.

The waiting hole swallowed the casket. And then, it was over. The crowd broke slowly. A few wandered off, a few more straggled away, then a large clump moved toward the parking lot.

One old man stared at me. The woman with him whispered something. I could almost read her lips. "That was Don's best friend," she was saying. The man nodded. They must have thought I was too overcome with grief to leave my car.

And that was it. *Good-bye, Don. Sorry I didn't watch the end, but we were together for a lot of good stuff.*

Life went on.

Within a week, Nick and Jennie became the hot couple. Heads turned when the two of them passed down the halls. I've heard that girls like a guy with a sense of humor. Nick certainly had that. He could even get most of the teachers to laugh. Once, he'd made Ms. Weldon laugh in the middle of a sip of coffee. She nearly choked.

The only teacher who never laughed was Mr. Loomis.

I remember the time he said, "Nick, I don't get your jokes. They're just not funny."

Without blinking, without even pausing for a second, Nick shot back at him with, "Maybe you should take my class. It's called *Humor for Teachers.*"

That cost him a week of detention. He didn't seem to mind. He joked about that, too: "Detention was great. What a learning experience. By the end of the week, I'd learned how to hot-wire a car, synthesize amphetamines, and buy a fake ID."

Time passed.

I went on a couple of dates with different girls, but it all felt like nothing more than going through the motions. I hung out with other friends. The hole Don had left didn't grow any smaller, but it moved further from the surface of my mind. I guess that's the way the mind heals the really bad wounds. More time passed. Looking back, three things stuck in my memory. The first happened about a month after Don's funeral. I think it was right after math class. My pen had leaked during class, so I stopped on my way down the hall to wash my hands. I ran into Nick in the bathroom.

"Hey, you and Jennie are going out," I said, just making empty conversation.

"Nope. We're staying in." Nick replied, making a typical speed-of-light response. He was out of the bathroom before I figured out the joke.

Maybe ten days after that, I passed him in the cafeteria. He was by himself. I guess Jennie had a class or something. She never seemed to join him for lunch. As I was walking by, Lou Watkins said to him, "So, you and Jennie getting serious?"

I paused to catch his response. I was sure it would be hilarious. But all he said was "Yeah, I suppose." He almost sounded sad.

The third thing happened less than a week later. I was in chemistry and had reached for a beaker on the Bunsen burner before giving it enough of a chance to cool down. I'd yelled, tossed it clumsily from hand to hand, and ended up dropping it on the floor. As I blew on my fingers, I glanced over to my left and noticed Nick. He'd seen my whole juggling act. I knew he'd cut me up with some sort of comment.

But he didn't say a word.

Maybe those three things wouldn't have stuck with

me, except for what happened next. That same evening, at 9:47, Nick Ferrano killed himself.

No joke.

Less than two months after they'd buried my best friend, I found myself at another funeral. It wasn't as bad. I guess the second time through anything is never as bad as the first. And to be honest, Nick wasn't a close friend. He was just a guy I knew. He was just a guy who used to make us all laugh.

Different church, same rituals. I sat near the back, knowing I would duck out this time and not even pretend to go to the cemetery.

"It's so very sad." Jennie slipped into the seat next to me. The room grew warmer. She was wearing the same black dress she'd worn at Don's funeral. For a moment—longer, I'm sure, than was proper—I admired her from up close. She didn't seem to mind.

"He . . ." I tried to get my thoughts together. "He had everything to live for."

"Yes," she said. She put her hand on my leg.

A shock ran from my knee to my groin. Part of me

wanted to hold her and bury my face in her hair. Part of me would have been happy to die in her arms.

"Were you two close?" she asked.

I shook my head. "We were in a lot of the same classes. I guess I knew him since sixth grade, but we weren't best friends or anything."

She looked right into my eyes. I had a strange feeling that I was taking a test. Her own eyes, her lovely eyes, seemed to reach into my heart.

"I need to walk," she said. "Will you walk with me when the service is over?"

"Sure."

So we strolled from the church and talked and agreed to meet the next day. I'm not sure how it happened, or who asked the other out. But it seemed that I was going to have a date with Jennie.

"Do you like movies?" she asked as we were discussing what to do.

"Yeah, usually," I said, hoping she wouldn't want to go to a horror film. Two of the five movies showing at the mall were horror. "What would you like to see?"

She smiled. "You choose."

I chose a comedy. It probably wouldn't have mattered

what we saw. I really didn't pay much attention to the movie, not with Jennie sitting next to me. As we left the theater, I asked her, "Want to grab a burger or something?"

She shook her head. "I'd better get home. But let's do something tomorrow. Okay?"

"I'd like that."

"Me, too. I had a really nice time with you." She smiled and touched my cheek for a moment with her warm, soft fingers. She seemed happy to be with me.

On our second date, half-afraid I'd destroy the magic by dissecting it, I asked her, "Why me?"

"Most boys are so dull," she'd answered. "You have something special inside. I can tell."

That didn't make much sense. I didn't feel special. But I didn't press her for an explanation. I wasn't going to reveal that all I had inside me was a lifetime of irrational fears. I wasn't going to lose her by exposing my flaws. I dropped the subject.

And just like that, we became the couple who turned heads. I guess people wondered what a stunning girl like Jennie was doing with someone like me. Not that I was a loser or a nerd or anything, but I certainly wasn't going to be voted most popular, or any of the other de-sirable mosts. Maybe "most likely to pass unnoticed" or "most average."

Average guys didn't date girls like Jennie. But there I was. And I wasn't going to question my luck. As much as I liked to know answers, as much as I always tried to find the reason behind things, I didn't risk asking her again.

And there were other things to wonder about.

It was funny. We spent a lot of time sitting in my car, just parked and talking. At first, I was so distracted by dark thoughts that I'm sure I rambled and babbled like an idiot. I especially remember one evening when I looked out the side window past Jennie's head, sud-denly thinking of that ridiculous story children tell—the one about the guy with the razor-sharp hook in place of a hand.

"What's the matter?" Jennie asked. "You seem dis-tracted."

"Nothing." How could I tell her?

"I like it here," she said. "It's so dark and quiet."

"Yeah. Sure. But sometimes . . ." I wanted to tell her,

but I couldn't. I waited for her to question me, to ask again. But she said nothing more about it.

A week later, at the same spot, I found myself caught again in thought. But this time, I paused in surprise when I realized that no dark images had spoiled our evening. For an hour or more, as we sat and talked and kissed, I'd not been visited by thoughts of razor-sharp hooks or walking corpses.

Maybe I was getting used to being out in the night with her. Maybe Jennie was giving me new confidence. The perfect example is almost too embarrassing to explain. We'd decided to rent a movie. We were going to watch it at my house. Jennie was kind of funny about that. I think she didn't want me to meet her parents. I wasn't sure whether it was because of me or because of them.

There were two video stores in town. I don't like the one near my house. They have an old cardboard figure of Freddy Krueger in the front aisle. I knew this was ridiculous, but I always got a little shiver when I walked past it, as if I felt it would spring to life and slash me. I guess I was sort of like Don that way, except he was always trying to avoid real dangers while I was trying to avoid the demons that sprang from my mind. Don would avoid walking across a storm grating because it might break while he was on it. I'd avoid the grating because something might reach through from below and drag me into the moist depths of the sewers. So, because of that stupid cardboard figure, I usually went to the other store to rent videos.

Then, one day, on the way home from school, I found myself driving past the video store with Jennie.

"Let's get a movie," she said.

"There's another place down the road," I told her. It was almost a reflex. I was used to coming up with quick excuses to mask my fears.

She put her hand on my arm. "That place never has the new movies. They have a better selection here."

"I guess they do." I circled the block and parked in front. As we walked into the shop and up the aisle, I noticed that the tremor, the subtle undercurrent of fright, was missing. I stopped to look at the cardboard figure. I didn't see something that was going to leap to life and shred me—I saw nothing more than a slightly blurred life-size photograph of an actor with a nice makeup job.

I took Jennie's hand as we strolled through the store. "I like being with you," I told her.

"I get so much from being with you, too," she said.

Over the next month, the little rituals, the small acts that paid tribute to my fears, began to vanish. I didn't have to make sure my feet were under the blanket. Half-asleep, I didn't worry about what might lurk beneath the bed. I know—that's stuff for five-year-old boys. Guys my age are over fears of monsters. But I couldn't help what I was.

Until now. Now, since I'd met Jennie, those things had started to fade. I'd found something else to fill my mind. Now that the fears were visiting my thoughts less frequently, I was very glad I'd never told her my secret. I doubt she would have thought much of me if she had known. She would never have wanted to be with someone who saw creatures in every shadow.

I didn't realize how much the fears had faded until the night we went to the cemetery.

"Let's go see Don's grave," Jennie said as we drove from the parking lot at the mall.

"What?" I felt my hands grip the wheel.

"He was your friend. Let's go pay our respects."

"But . . ."

She put her hand on top of mine. "Come on, he needs to be remembered."

I took a deep breath. Then I thought, *Sure, why not?* We parked outside. The gate was locked at night. I helped Jennie over the fence, lingering to enjoy the feel of my hands on her hips. She hopped down gracefully, then waited until I joined her.

Jennie took my hand and led me through the maze of marble headstones. I kept glancing at the graves, waiting for the images to take over my mind, waiting for my brain to fill with scenes of rotting hands exploding through the soil to clutch at our legs and pull us down to join them. My mind seemed dead to such fears.

We reached Don's grave. There was no headstone yet—I guess they take a while to make—but there was a marker on the ground with his name.

When we knelt on the ground, I braced myself, but there was no rush of dreadful images. There were no visions of corpses rising from below. All I felt was distant sadness.

When Jennie lay down and pulled me to her, all I felt

was lust and hunger. All else vanished as we kissed and wrapped our arms around each other.

My fears were gone.

"What do you feel?" she whispered.

I told her.

I returned to the cemetery the next evening, alone. The stories and images that had once haunted me now drew me. For an hour, I sat by Don's grave, sometimes talking to him, sometimes just thinking in silence.

"I never told you about this," I said. "It seems silly now, but I want you to know." I talked about the way I'd been. It felt good telling Don the truth.

But I was confessing my past, not my future. There was no fear in me. None at all. Nothing in this land of graves and death brought terror to my mind. To test myself, I wandered deeper into the cemetery. There was an open grave, empty, awaiting. With the strange belief that it was waiting for me, I climbed down inside it, feeling the trickle of soil fall from the edge to join me at the bottom. I lay flat on the damp earth and thought of being buried alive. It felt right. It felt good.

I imagined the earth dropping over me. First, a shovelful, spreading as it fell. Then another. Falling like thick rain, covering me, burying me alive.

The images didn't bring fear. They excited me.

Like a thirst, the need rose within me, bursting to the surface of my mind, grabbing me so hard that I sat up and scrambled from the grave.

I needed it to happen for real.

But where?

I searched through the cemetery, failed to find what I needed, then returned to the street. Up the road, I saw the lights of the old supermarket. Then I knew. I closed my eyes and thought of the gaping hole that had once filled me with dread. I had to go to the east side of town, where they were building the new supermarket. I'd slip in tonight and wait for morning. They were constantly moving earth, shoving piles of dirt from place to place. Within the rush of bulldozers and trucks and tons of earth, they'd never notice me.

It would be easy.

I got in my car and drove, looking forward to the feel of the earth as it covered my still-breathing body.

A car at the cross street ran a stop sign. I hit the

brakes. My tires squealed, the rear end fishtailed, but I stopped in time. The shoulder belt pressed against my chest, like the hand of a friend trying to keep me from harm.

Don would have had a fit if he was with me, I thought.

But Don was dead.

Nick would have said something funny.

But Nick was dead.

I started to move my foot from the brake.

My leg froze. Don and Jennie. Nick and Jennie. Me and Jennie. I remembered another moment like this. It was three days before Don had died. We were riding to the city so Don could get a present for Jennie at this fancy gift shop. I'd jammed on the brakes after deciding at the last moment not to run a light. Don had leaned pretty far forward. He couldn't have moved that far unless he hadn't been wearing his seat belt. I tried to remember the details, but they were hazy. I tried to think of other moments from Don's last month.

Small things came back, things I'd seen but not really been aware of before. Don cutting an apple, slicing toward himself with a sharp knife. Don running down a flight of stairs. I saw it now—Don had grown less and less cautious over the last few months. Finally, he'd lost all his caution, and his life.

I did a U-turn and headed toward Jennie's house. Something was forming in my mind. It wasn't easy to think. I still wanted to embrace a suffocating mound of earth.

It was late. I hoped her parents wouldn't mind. I'd never met them. Jennie always waited for me in front. She never invited me in. I guess the time had come for that meeting.

I knocked at the door.

After a long while, Jennie answered. She seemed surprised to see me. Then she spoke, and it was my turn to be surprised.

"Weren't you going somewhere?" she asked. "Don't you have something you need to do?"

"Yes," I said, too surprised to deny my plans. I took a step inside. The room was empty except for a chair. There was no way to tell from where I stood, but I sensed that the rest of the house was also empty, both of furniture and parents. I suspected Jennie had been on her own for a long time.

She stroked my cheek. "Tell me what you want," she

said. She dropped her arm quickly, as if the touch meant nothing. "Tell me what you need."

"To be buried," I said. "To end my days beneath tons of earth. Buried but still alive. Alive, but knowing there is nothing ahead except death." Even the sound of it excited me. Combined with the lingering feel of her touch, it was almost more than I could bear.

"Go. It's waiting for you." Her voice was like a soft caress against the most sensitive folds of my brain.

Yes. Of course. She was right. My Jennie knew what I needed to do. I turned to leave. Behind me, I heard a sound—perhaps a sigh of relief. I turned back. "What are you?" I asked.

She smiled. "Surely you know. You've touched me, felt me. I've had no secrets from you."

I didn't understand. But I had to understand. I waited for her to speak again.

"You took what you wanted. I took what I needed. I'm like you—we all feed on each other. But you're empty. You have nothing more for me. Go to your destiny."

What did she take? Fighting the urge to run to my car, I tried to think. I began to see the pattern. Don had been robbed of his caution. Nick had been robbed of his humor. Each had lost—as it hit me, I spoke aloud. "The strongest feeling . . ."

She said nothing.

I knew. From each, she had taken the part that had been the strongest. She had stolen my fears. Just as she had stolen Don's caution, leaving him to run across a highway no sane person would try to cross. She had stolen Nick's humor, leaving him empty of life. No reason to laugh, no reason to live. Whatever remained—the bones, the pits, the peelings—was thrown in the garbage. Jennie had chosen each of us because we had so much for her to take. Then she'd drained us.

"Do you know what you've stolen from me?"

She shrugged. "I didn't pay that much attention."

My hands clenched into fists. As bad as it was to have been robbed, it was almost worse that she didn't seem to know or care what she had stolen. "Don't you even know what you have taken?"

"Can you tell me what you had for breakfast last week?" she asked. "That's all you were to me. An egg. A bowl of cereal. A piece of meat. Nothing more. I'm interested in my next meal, not my last one. A girl like me has to plan ahead. You young ones are most tasty. Your emotions and feelings are so strong."

Slowly, she licked her lips. "I think it's time for me to move to another town. I almost left after the last one. Nick? I think that was his name. I almost left, but you were so very hard to resist. So full and juicy."

I stared at her, with no idea what to do. She'd stolen my fears of the imagined and the unseen. Under any other circumstances, that would have been a huge favor. But now I was supposed to follow Don and Nick. To her, I was nothing but the inedible scraps and gristle left after a two-month feast. Still, I had to know. "What are you?"

Jennie smiled. "This happens sometimes. Once in a while, the waste refuses to flush itself. That's not a problem. I'll show you. It's kind of fun—for me. But you won't survive. Your heart will burst. Your brain will drown in blood from exploded veins."

She stepped back several paces. "Are you sure you wouldn't rather go to your destiny?"

"No."

"Last chance."

"Show me."

She shimmered. She shifted. She stood before me as she really was. Maybe. Perhaps this was her true form. Perhaps it was just an illusion she could cast as her ultimate protection. Before me, a creature unlike man or woman stood. Ancient, dry, and withered, with insect eyes in a skull of wrinkled, flaking flesh. Small at first, hunched, no more than four feet tall.

She rose. Her skeleton extended as she grew five, then six, then seven feet. Her arms spread, glistening chitinous wings draped from ribs to elbows. Her face alone would have stopped the heart of anyone who looked upon it. Her weapon was fear. She could scare mortals to death, turn them to stone like a modern Medusa.

But I was empty of fear.

Anyone else would have died at the sight of her. This was her ultimate weapon. But she had dined on my fear and stolen it from me.

"Guess what? You don't scare me." I stepped forward. My foot struck a hard object. I reached down, needing to grip something real. My hands met wood. I grabbed the chair and swung it at her. I was empty of fear, but I had rage. I had rage and anger and strength. The chair smashed against her. She crumpled as she rammed into a wall, then slowly stood again. Something thick and brown oozed from the side of her head. It smelled like burning hair and rotting flesh. I swung again. The chair shattered in my hands. I leaped on her, this time with a lust for vengeance.

I seized her neck—or whatever it was that led from head to body—and squeezed and shook. The flesh felt dry and brittle.

Her mouth opened. Her jaw unhinged like the jaw of a snake. Pieces of what she had stolen from her victims splashed over me like acid. Remnants of the strongest feelings and emotions of hundreds of her victims spilled from her.

Perhaps some of my own fear returned. I grew afraid enough to open my hands and let her head drop to the floor. It hit with the sound of a straw basket dropped on concrete.

But by then she was dead.

I stood and looked at the mess of fragile bones and skin and other things I never wanted to know about. It didn't look like anything that could be mistaken for human remains. Already, it was crumbling, losing its identity among the dust and dirt on the floor.

"For Don," I said as I stood and backed slowly away from the spot. "For Nick. For all of them. And for me."

I left the house and walked to my car. The night was dark and still and, within the deep shadows, a little bit frightening. But it was nothing I couldn't face. Nothing I couldn't handle.

Every Drop

The sun had burned off the faintest wisps of clouds and beat down without mercy. It was the first truly hot afternoon in July.

"Perfect day for swimming," Jake said as he checked the road to make sure no cars were coming. He slipped through the hole someone had cut ages ago in the fence beneath the KEEP OUT sign. A narrow path, worn down by countless feet, led him toward the south side of the old reservoir. Two more signs nailed to trees along the path also warned him to keep out.

He didn't see anyone else there when he stepped into the small clearing near the bank. No surprise. It was still early in the afternoon. Jake stripped down to his underwear, then leaned out to grab the rope that hung from a branch of one of the maple trees that lined the bank. He swung out, let go, and plunged into the cool water.

He swam for a while, then pulled himself out of the water and dropped to the grass just as he heard footsteps coming through the brush. *Hope it's Sheryl,* he thought. It would be nice watching her, or any of the other hot girls, splashing around in the water.

"Hey, what's happening?" an annoying voice called out.

Oh, crap. Jake glanced up, barely acknowledging the greeting with a nod of his head.

Rodney Werner stepped from the path. Jake noticed the nerd was wearing a bathing suit and carrying a towel. How lame could a guy get?

"You been here long?" he asked.

Jake grunted, hoping the jerk would take a hint and go pollute some other spot along the bank.

But Rodney walked right up to him. "The sun's actually farther away from the earth in the summer than in the winter. Did you know that?"

Jake didn't even bother grunting. One of the great joys of Rodney was that he had a zillion mind-numbing bits of information to share, and no clue how uninterested the rest of the planet was in hearing any of it.

Rodney took a deep breath, then said, "I might have just inhaled the very same molecule that was breathed by Julius Caesar. Imagine that. The same air that Caesar breathed. Across centuries and miles."

Just kill me now, Jake thought.

"I love water. Our bodies are ninety percent water.

Did you know that? Some trees like to be near water." Rodney pointed to the maple tree. "That's a red maple. Most people can't tell them from sugar maples." His hand dropped as he pointed to the spot next to Jake. "Hey, mind if I join you? This is great. I was afraid there'd be nobody here."

Jake's mind searched for the best way to tell Rodney to take a hike. He wanted the guy to go as far away as possible. Like over to the other side. As Jake glanced across the water, he got an idea that was so sweet, he had to struggle to keep from smirking.

"Actually, I was about to swim. Want to race?"

"Sure." Roddy looked toward the water. "How far?"

"All the way."

"Are you kidding?"

"Hey, it's easy. I already did it once today. It's not as far as it looks. Anyone can make it. Anyone with guts." He got up and walked toward the edge of the bank. "Ready?"

As Roddy stood there with his mouth open, Jake yelled, "Go!" and dived into the water. He stroked along for a couple of yards, then pulled to the surface, swimming slowly and listening. A couple of seconds later, he heard the loud splash of a clumsy dive. As he continued to swim slowly toward the distant bank, he saw Roddy catch up. Jake kept pace with him for a couple more strokes and then lagged, letting Roddy get ahead.

Once Rodney was well past him, Jake stopped to tread water. Roddy was still going, obviously clueless that he was in a one-man race. Jake turned and swam back to the shore. "Jerk," he muttered as he climbed back on the bank.

Jake watched, expecting Roddy to turn back way before he reached the middle. But the fool kept going. The water churned around him as he beat at it with his awkward strokes. *Sucker's going to make it,* Jake thought. He grinned at the idea of Rodney climbing onto the other shore and then turning around. The geek would scan the water first, and then, after a while, he'd finally notice Jake waving from the other side.

Good joke.

Rodney was about twenty yards away from the far bank when his stroke changed. It slowed, then stopped. He started to thrash.

Jake ran to the edge of the water. There was no point trying to swim across. He knew he'd never get there in time to help. Assuming he could even make it that far. He'd never work his way around the bank, either. There were too many overgrown spots.

By the time he'd thought all this through, Rodney had sunk from sight.

Jake stared across the reservoir. *I don't need this kind of problem,* he thought. *Rodney should have been smart enough not to try that.* It was Rodney's own fault, Jake realized. Darwinism in action. Survival of the coolest. He glanced around again. Nobody else had seen anything.

Though Jake kept his mouth shut, even a geek like Rodney was eventually missed. The alarms went out. Posters went up. Local news crews came by for a day or two. But he was old enough that everyone figured he was another runaway. Jake shoved the whole thing out of his mind, feeling less and less connected to the drowning with each passing day. But he also avoided the old reservoir.

The heat remained brutal through July, and the sky remained cloudless. Toward the end of the month, waking late in the morning, Jake got a glass of water from the kitchen. As he drank, he glanced down at the paper on the table. WATER LEVEL LOW, the headline said. Below that, CITY TAPS OLD RESERVOIR FOR BACKUP.

Jake's body jerked as a mouthful of water sloshed toward his lungs. He coughed, spraying water across the kitchen. His body convulsed as if he were drowning. He put the glass down, forced himself to take deep breaths, and waited for the feeling to fade.

When he was back in control, he stared at the glass. "Don't be stupid," he muttered. The reservoir water was filtered and sanitized and mixed with all sorts of chemicals. It was perfectly safe to drink.

He picked up the glass, feeling just as he had the first time, and the last, he tried sushi. He took a small sip and swallowed carefully.

Not carefully enough. The water went the wrong way, sending him into another fit of coughing.

Five hours later, when his thirst was more than he could bear, he got a glass of milk from the fridge. The first tiny sip went down fine. So did the rest. There was nothing wrong with his ability to swallow. Before he went to bed, he tried the water again. He choked immediately.

"No big deal," he said. He'd drink milk, juice, and soda.

The next morning, the water in the shower stung like needles. No matter how he adjusted the showerhead, he couldn't make it comfortable. Jake washed as quickly as he could and got out.

A week later, he choked for the first time on a glass of milk. Jake looked at the label on the carton. The dairy was over in a nearby town. Fed by the same reservoir.

The soda, he soon discovered, was bottled in his city. He drank spring water. Problem solved. But he started choking on foods. Anything cooked in water. Anything mixed with water.

By early August, he knew he had to get away. At least for a while. Long enough for the last of the tainted water to leave the reservoir. He got permission to go visit his cousin in Texas. It was only a two-day drive.

Jake got started late. He figured he'd drive through the night, catch a couple of hours' sleep the next day, and then push on. The air was damp when he got in his car.

Ten minutes after he left his house, the first drop hit his windshield. Jake turned on his wipers, then turned them off. The blade just smeared the scattered drops across the glass, obscuring his view.

The rain started to fall more heavily. He switched on the wipers again. The water smeared worse, turning the view through the windshield into a mosaic of dark patches and soft blurs of light.

Jake switched the wipers to the highest speed. It didn't help. He couldn't see at all. He rolled down his window and tried looking out to see the road. The rain stung his eyes and lashed at his face. *Better pull over,* he thought. He wiped his face, then reached out for the switch to close the window. The car drifted to the right. Through the half-closed window, barely visible through the heavy rain, Jake spotted the thin white line marking the shoulder of the road. It curved sharply to the left. As Jake jammed his foot on the brake and yanked the wheel, he felt the car lurch. The tires skidded on the wet pavement.

He was off the road. Relieved that he hadn't been going too fast, Jake waited for the car to stop.

It slowed. But it was tilted too far. It started to roll. It seemed to take forever. Jake held on. *I'll be okay,* he thought. The car rolled on its side and then onto its roof. Instead of a scrape of rocks and dirt, Jake heard a splash.

As rain fell around him in torrents, the car started to sink in the swollen stream. Jake yanked open the buckle of his seat belt. A million knives slashed at him as water flooded through the half-open window. Jake took a deep breath, then forced his head through the opening. He jammed his shoulders through.

His hips stuck. Water surrounded his head, searing his eyes like acid. He jerked with strength driven by panic and managed to pull free of the car.

The current tugged at him, trying to sweep him toward the middle of the creek. Jake swam. "Screw you, Rodney!" he screamed. Rage fueled his strokes. His hand met the twisted root of a tree. He held on, catching his breath, letting his strength return before he tried to climb up the steep bank. He was a survivor, no matter what the odds.

A phrase flashed through his memory. *The same air that Ceasar breathed.* Those molecules had spread throughout the world.

The same water that Rodney breathed. Or the same water that Rodney was.

It would be everywhere. In every bottle. In every glass. In every cloud. Every stream or ocean or puddle. Every wisp of fog. Water, water, everywhere.

There was no way he could win. Jake's fingers slipped loose. The current dragged him away, and then pulled him under. He opened his mouth to swear. Water filled his throat. It dashed eagerly into his lungs and tugged at his body. It carried him away, swirling toward the rivers and the oceans.

The alarms went out. Posters went up. Local news crews came by for a day or two. But nobody really cared.

Patterns of Fear

Collin scanned the table as they all took their seats. It was exactly what he'd expected: beauty, fear, humor, beefcake, and logic. It was the same pattern as always. A gorgeous girl who looked like she'd popped off the cover of a magazine. A mousy girl who looked like she'd start crying if he shouted, "Boo!" A goofy-looking guy who was there for comic relief. A male model who probably had an IQ somewhere below that of a fried egg. And him. The cool, calm, logical sort. The brains of the operation. As always.

"Fear comes from ignorance," he'd said during the interview with the producer last month. The man seemed impressed with that, so Collin had gone on to discuss his feelings about the unknown and the unexplained. It had worked. He got the job. He'd tried out for the show on a whim. And now, here he was, with the rest of the group who'd star in an episode of *Terror at Midnight*.

What a joke, Collin thought. The show, which traveled around the country, was a rip-off of the one on MTV. And that was pretty much ripped off from a movie, anyhow.

But the money wasn't a rip-off. A sweet five-hundred-dollar payday for each one of them who stayed all night. And a chance to make bonus money.

"All set?" the producer asked.

Collin nodded along with the others. The producer introduced everyone, but Collin didn't bother learning any names. They'd be together for only one night. And he already had perfect names for them: Barbie, Minnie, Dufus, and Sergio.

The producer led them to a Honda in the parking lot. "Here you go," he said, dangling a set of keys attached to a small rubber skeleton.

"I'll drive," Sergio said, snatching the keys.

"No camera crew?" Barbie asked.

"It's all automated, babe," the producer said. "The cameras are in place throughout the house."

And in the car, Collin thought. That way they'd get some good shots of the group as they marked their territory.

"What about the bathrooms?" Minnie asked.

"Relax, doll. We aren't that kind of show."

Sergio headed for the driver's side. "Shotgun!" Dufus shouted, grabbing the front passenger seat.

"Moron," Collin muttered, quietly enough so nobody

heard him. He was pleased with the seating arrange-ments. "I'll take the middle," he said. "I don't mind." He didn't mind at all. Barbie might have been an airhead, but he'd certainly enjoy having her squeezed in next to him.

The rest of them chattered as Sergio drove along, fol-lowing instructions from the tape in the cassette player.

Collin had to admit that this was a clever gimmick.

"Creepy," Minnie said when they pulled through the tilted iron gates that waited for them at the end of the ride.

"Rrrrrrrrrr." Dufus did a creaky-gate impression. Bar-bie sighed. Minnie let out a nervous giggle.

Sergio drove along the curving driveway.

Everyone except Collin let out a gasp when they reached the house. They sat for a moment, then opened the car doors and climbed out. Their breaths drifted be-fore them in the frigid night. The place was exactly what Collin would have expected if someone had cast around for the perfect haunted house. A crumbling old Victorian. Three stories. Dangling shutters that probably flapped against the sides when the wind picked up. A dead tree in the front yard. *Nice touch,* Collin thought. Flaking black paint. Drawn curtains in the windows.

Collin hung back as the group headed toward the

steps. He'd started watching the show after getting the job. It always had the same pattern. The Sergio-of-the-Week would rush up the steps first to show how brave he was. Barbie would follow. Dufus would chase after her, making lame jokes. Finally, he'd have to talk Minnie into coming along. That was his role. The voice of reason. He knew the viewers would be rooting for him to turn tail and run. Everyone liked to see the rational person succumb to fear. Not a chance.

"It's so creepy." Minnie stood with her arms wrapped around herself.

"It's just a house," Collin told her. He could swear he heard her teeth chattering. "There's nothing spooky or supernatural inside. You'll be fine. The only thing to worry about is dust."

"I'm allergic."

So don't breathe. He herded her up the steps and they went inside.

A cassette player waited for them on a table in the hallway. Sergio pushed the PLAY button.

"Welcome to Morimar House," the recorded voice said. "It's haunted. The locals agree on that. What they can't agree on is whether it is merely malicious or deeply evil. Perhaps the five of you will find an answer for us. If you stay . . ."

The narrator chuckled, then said, "Now, let us begin our tour."

Sergio picked up the cassette player and led the group through the house.

Every time a board creaked under their feet, Minnie squeaked. *I hope she's the first to leave,* Collin thought. On most shows, at least two of the team backed out. Sometimes, all of them fled. Not this time. Collin knew he'd be there when the sun came up and the check-book came out.

The tour took them to the basement, and then through each of the three floors. Finally, they went up a long flight of steep stairs to the attic.

As Sergio opened the door and they followed him in, Collin had a surprise. It wasn't Minnie who whimpered. It was Dufus. "I can't do this," he said. He backed out of the room. "I'm not going in there."

That was enough to spook Minnie, who joined him in the hall.

"It's just another room," Collin said. He glanced at the others. Sergio and Barbie looked like they'd been joined at the hip. "Just a room," Collin repeated. An old, ragged rug covered the floor. The sloping ceiling barely allowed him enough room to stand. A bed with a wooden headboard was pushed against the far wall. A bare bulb with a pull cord hung over the bed. There were two plump pillows. The kind that were probably stuffed with feathers. And a large quilt. Bed, pillows, and quilt all looked pretty old.

The only furniture was a small table by the bed, a wooden chair, and a dresser with a mirror.

Someone had pasted magazine pictures on one of the walls. Flowers. Birds. All sorts of cheerful stuff.

Collin shivered. But not from fear. The house was cold. Especially the attic. Much colder than it was downstairs. That didn't make sense. Heat rose. He knew that. Maybe the rest of the house was better insulated. That would explain it. Whatever warmth there was had been trapped below.

"Let's get out of here," Barbie said.

Collin followed them downstairs. They built a fire in the fireplace. Naturally, Sergio took charge of it. Five sleeping bags lay unrolled by the hearth. On each one, there was an envelope with a name.

Collin picked up his. Inside, on a file card, it said,

Challenge—sleep alone in the basement.

Reward—$500.

He glanced at the others as they read their cards. Each had been offered money to stay alone in a selected room. The money varied. Sergio's was the highest. One thousand dollars to sleep in the attic.

Figures they'd give the big bucks to the pretty boy. "We can trade," Collin said. That was one of the rules of the show. He knew what he wanted. Why settle for an extra five hundred dollars when he could get one thousand?

"I'm not sleeping alone," Barbie said. She held out her card. "Anyone want it?"

Collin shook his head. He wasn't interested in three hundred dollars for sleeping in the kitchen. But he knew what would come next. "You won't be alone. I'll keep you company," Sergio said. He tossed his card to the floor.

"You mind?" Collin asked.

Sergio shrugged. "The less, the merrier."

Collin took the card.

"Aren't you afraid?" Minnie asked.

"Of what?"

"That's a bad place," Dufus said.

"Route 22 at rush hour is a bad place," Collin said. "The attic is just a room." He couldn't help smiling. Not only was he smarter than Dufus, he was funnier, too. He hoped the audience would appreciate his wit. But he figured anyone who watched *Terror at Midnight* probably wasn't bright enough to enjoy real humor.

The group had to stay together until midnight. Collin sat on the floor and let the others do the talking. It didn't matter. He'd get paid even if he didn't say another word.

At twelve, they all said good night. Collin trudged up toward the attic. He left the sleeping bag behind. The bed looked a lot more comfortable. But as he walked along the last hallway and climbed the steps, he wished he'd brought it, just to drape over himself until he got to the room. It was even colder now.

Nothing spooky here, he thought as he went inside. He kicked off his shoes and pulled down the quilt. *Weird,* he thought as he glanced at it. There didn't seem to be much of a pattern. Just scraps of cloth. Obviously made to serve a purpose and not to please the eye.

Comfy, Collin thought as he pressed his hand into one of the pillows.

When he got in bed, he noticed a scrapbook on the bedside table. The first entry, a clipping so old that the paper looked ready to turn to dust, said, MURDER IN THE ATTIC.

Nice touch. Collin decided to be a sport and read the article out loud. He wasn't sure where the camera was hidden, but he knew there'd be one somewhere.

According to the article, the place used to be a guest-house. The first owner had killed his wife by smothering her with a pillow. Way back in 1893. Collin felt a small twinge in his stomach. He reached behind himself and pulled out one of the pillows. It was too new. And there was a tag on it. He wouldn't be sleeping with his face pressed against a murder weapon.

The place changed hands, but remained a guest-house.

The next clipping, dated 1907, told of a visitor who had apparently died of fright while sleeping in the attic. The doctor described him as "paralyzed by such extreme fear that his face was frozen in the most ghastly expression."

Heart attack, Collin thought. Doctors didn't know much

back in 1907. They were probably still using leeches. He flipped the page.

Three more clippings told of similar deaths—two from fright and one labeled "accidental strangulation." The next, dated 1957, told about a young girl who had leaped from the window.

Collin glanced over at the window. It was covered with boards. Nailed solidly shut. *Not me,* he said. Even if the window was wide open, he'd never jump. There were more clippings, but Collin had seen enough. Besides, he was pretty sure they were fake. It wouldn't be hard to make something look old like that. Forgers did it all the time. He slid down under the quilt, pulled the dusty old cloth up to his chin, then decided to say one more word for the benefit of the cameras. "G'night."

He yanked the cord that dangled from the bulb. The room dropped into complete blackness.

Collin closed his eyes.

He opened them an instant later when he heard the moan.

His hand shot for the cord. Then he froze. It was a trick. The producer had set something up.

The sound had faded. Collin felt pleased that he

hadn't panicked and turned on the light. They weren't going to trick him that easily.

The pleasure didn't last. It was replaced by panic when he felt a moist breath puff against his cheek.

Collin shouted. He fumbled for the light. Then instantly felt foolish as he blinked against the harsh glare. He touched his cheek. It had seemed so real. A breath, like a dying gasp, already scented with the grave.

No. It couldn't have been a breath. He raised the quilt slightly, then let it drop. A puff of air washed over his hand. That explained it. His only enemy was an overactive imagination.

Stay calm. Stay logical.

"Okay, what are the facts?" he said, speaking quietly. A bunch of people died in this room. So what? People died everywhere. Which meant, first of all, that it wasn't unusual that people died here, and second of all, that if places were haunted because people died there, then the whole freaking world would have to be haunted.

Logic. Rational thought. Find the patterns in the unexplained, and it was no longer unexplained.

And just this once, for no rational reason, leave the light on.

Collin started to lie back down. Then he decided that he really didn't need a pillow. He tossed them both on the floor. He closed his eyes.

And felt fingers on his throat.

Collin sat up. As his own scream faded, he heard another one. An old man. Half-screaming, half-sobbing in terror.

Tricks, Collin thought.

But the sound wasn't from a hidden speaker. It came from inside his head. Like a memory. But loud and undeniably real.

"Okay—I can deal with this," he said, not bothering to keep his voice down. Screw the cameras. He didn't care if his momentary panic was flashed on the screen for millions of viewers. Because in the end, he'd triumph. He'd find the rational explanation.

The voice in his head was fading. He drowned it out by speaking over it.

"Voices . . . How? Maybe drugs. Something in the food?" They'd been given dinner before heading out. "No. Not legal. There'd be trouble. Has to be something else. Hypnotism?" Maybe. That would explain it. Post-hypnotic suggestion. Some sort of audio-acoustic trick with high-tech speakers? Somehow, they'd tricked him into hearing sounds.

He walked over to the mirror, bracing himself for some gory sight. It wouldn't be hard to rig a projector. But all he saw was his own wide-eyed reflection.

Calm down. He pulled the pictures from the wall, hoping to uncover some sort of hidden mechanism. Nothing showed up.

Collin went back to bed.

The bed jolted like someone had kicked it.

Ancient springs creaked. The whole frame shook like someone was struggling. Fighting for breath.

Collin rolled off the bed, tangling himself in the quilt. He staggered but caught his balance, then knelt by the side of the bed and looked underneath. Nothing. He rolled back the rug, revealing a bare, untampered floor. He grunted as he pushed the mattress off the bed frame. The shaking had stopped.

"Hidden motors," he said. "Someone shaking the floor from the room below. Yeah. Tricks. Stupid tricks. Not real."

He heard glass break. Another scream. High pitched. Then fading. A distant thud—three floors down—ended the scream.

"The hell with this." Collin threw off the quilt as he rushed to the door. Five hundred dollars was enough. He'd camp out downstairs with the others. He didn't need the extra thousand. Not that badly.

He grabbed the knob, half-expecting that it would break off in his hand, trapping him in the attic. But the door opened easily.

He stepped onto the stairs, where a frigid blast of air rushed up to greet him. He hadn't gone more than two steps when he had a vision—not of ghosts from the past but of events from the near future that would be preserved forever on videotape. Sergio would laugh at him. Dufus would make jokes. Barbie would look at him like he was a pathetic loser. And, worst of all, Minnie would comfort him. *It's okay. We all get scared. It's nothing to be ashamed about.* The scared mouse would soothe the thinker.

No way. He looked back at the door. He didn't believe in haunted houses. But there was definitely something wrong inside that attic. He'd find another room. Too bad he couldn't build a fire. He'd seen no other fireplaces during the tour. No other beds, either.

But the quilt lay just beyond the doorway. Fighting

the image of a sharp-clawed hand snagging his arm, Collin leaned over and grabbed the quilt, then wrapped it around himself.

"Haunted attic," he muttered as he started down the steps. "Absurd." The deaths flashed through his mind. Smothered. *In bed.* Died of fright. *In bed.* Strangled. *In bed.*

It wasn't the attic. It was the bed. He glanced over his shoulder. The frame was now level with his eyes.

No. That was ridiculous. There was no such thing as a haunted bed.

He took another step.

What about the other one? How had that happened? He could see the girl leap from the bed and run toward the window. Fleeing the bed. By why not through the door? Why the window? What had forced her where she wouldn't want to go?

"Find the pattern," he said.

He could see her so clearly. Stumbling, staggering . . . Dragging the quilt.

The quilt.

In the dim light, Collin looked down at the patternless jumble of fabrics. And saw the patterns. The abstract shapes fell together. A man holding a pillow. The murder that had started all of this. He saw all the others that followed. A face bursting with fright. Another gasping for air as fabric wrapped tightly around his throat. An open window.

The quilt.

Screams of past victims flooded his mind. He struggled to tear the quilt loose, but his hands were trapped. The cloth pulled around him like a funeral shroud.

His feet tangled in the tightening quilt.

Collin tripped. He fell. Rolling, tumbling, screaming.

But he was silent when he landed.

The others, still awake and talking by the fire, came hesitantly up the steps. A moment later, they were joined by the production crew, which was monitoring everything from a trailer parked behind the house.

They stood and stared at the body. Nobody noticed, along one side of the quilt that had tangled around Collin, a colorful arrangement of cloth that, when viewed at just the right angle, seemed to show a man falling down a flight of stairs.

Nobody noticed any of the patterns.

Free Seas

Which boat is it?"

"Shhh. Quiet. It's Pace Cruise Lines," Steven whispered. He crouched down on the pier next to Mary.

"There. That's it," she said.

"Yeah. Good job." Steven felt a rush of adrenaline shoot through his gut when he realized they were going to do it. Not just talk and plan. Not just daydream. Really do it. There was the ship. He could see most of the name, except for a couple of letters that were blocked by a cargo crane. There was the P on the left, then the E on the other side of the crane arm, followed by CRUISE LINES. It was the ship Brennan Winston had told him about.

"Ready?" he asked Mary.

"You sure about this?" she asked.

"Yeah. It'll be awesome. We'll blend right in with the passengers. It's just for three days. But think about all that food and fun."

He crept toward the ship, trying to move silently on the old wood of the pier. He could hear Mary slipping along behind him. All they had to do was sneak down below and hide. Brennan had told him how to do it.

"It's real dark," Mary complained as they made their way up the walkway and onto the ship.

"Shhh. The passengers aren't boarding until tomorrow morning. Just follow me." Steven led Mary down below.

"What if we get caught?" Mary asked when they reached the bottom of the lowest deck, guided only by dim night-lights.

"I told you, they won't do anything. We're minors. They'll just wait until the boat gets back to the dock and make us leave. Keep calm and they won't catch us. Okay?" Steven reached out and gave her arm a squeeze.

"Okay," Mary said. "I guess. . . ."

The rocking of the boat woke Steven the next morning. "Hey, we made it," he said, nudging Mary's shoulder.

She sat up fast, looking startled, and he had to shush her again. "I need a bathroom," she said.

"No problem," Steven told her. "Put on your suit and we'll go up on deck."

Mary pulled off her shorts and top, revealing she'd worn her suit underneath. Steven grabbed his from his backpack. He noticed that Mary turned around when he changed. *She'll get over it,* he told himself.

"Now be cool," he said. "We belong here. Just keep that in mind and nobody will pay any attention to us." He opened the door and peeked out. There wasn't anyone in the hallway. As long as they weren't spotted coming out of the storage room, there'd be no problem.

Steven braced himself to meet people. He knew the first moments would be the toughest. But all he had to do was nod and smile, or just ignore the other passengers. That would work. Adults expected to be ignored by teens. *You're on vacation,* he reminded himself.

They didn't meet anyone as they climbed the steps from level to level.

"Must be early," Steven said.

There was nobody on deck.

"This is wrong." Mary grabbed his arm. "This is really strange."

"Relax," Steven said, though he had to fight to keep the calm tone in his voice.

"It's a ghost ship!" Mary stepped away from him and spun around, as if searching for something to prove her wrong.

"Mary, stop acting crazy," Steven said. "There's no such thing as a ghost ship."

"Yes, there is. Look around. There's nobody here. Nobody. Just us." She ran back down the stairs toward the cabins.

Steven cursed and ran after her. He knew he had to calm her down before she got them both in trouble. He managed to catch up with her halfway down the corridor. "Wait. Look, everything is fine. I'll prove it to you."

He reached for the nearest doorknob, frantically trying to figure out what to do once he opened the door and came face-to-face with strangers. He realized he could just pretend he had the wrong cabin. That would work. And Mary would see that everything was fine. So would he.

Steven gripped the knob of cabin A37. He figured that the doors were probably locked. But even that might help Mary realize there were people on the other side.

The knob turned smoothly in his hand.

Steven eased the door open and peeked inside. An old guy was lying on the bed, fast asleep.

"See?" Steven whispered.

He waited until Mary nodded, then shut the door. "Look. It must be early. That's why everyone's still asleep.

Come on. Let's see if they've put out any breakfast yet. I'm starving."

They went back up.

There was no food.

No waiters.

No crew.

"This is crazy," Steven said. He looked around the deck. Then he looked toward the ocean. There was no land in sight. They were far out at sea. "When we get back, I'm going to tell Brennan that Pace Cruise Lines sucks."

Mary let out a small whimper.

"What now?" Steven asked. He was starting to wish he'd asked someone else to come with him.

"It's not Pace," Mary said.

"Huh?" Steven wondered why she was whispering.

Mary didn't answer him. She pointed up at a mast above them. Steven noticed her hand was shaking.

Fluttering overhead, a flag displayed the name, PYRE CRUISE LINES.

"Pyre," Steven said. English wasn't his best subject. The word took a minute to register. When it did, he knew that the man he'd seen in the cabin below wasn't asleep. The man was dead.

Everyone on the ship was dead.

Pyre. As in *funeral pyre.*

Music began to play over loudspeakers. Slow, sad music. Beneath his feet, Steven heard the crackle of flames and felt the rising heat of the fire.

In the distance, Steven saw another ship. Squinting, he could make out the name PACE CRUISE LINES on the side. Dots of moving color told him that people were frolicking on deck, having the vacation of a lifetime.

Mary screamed.

The pyre grew. Steven turned to run, but there were flames everywhere.

"Look?" the first mate asked the passenger, offering his binoculars.

"Thanks," the man said. He peered across the water at the rising flames. "Wow. Pretty spectacular. What a way to go."

The mate nodded. "Yeah. At least they're feeling no pain." He stood at the deck and watched as the burning funeral ship slowly drifted into the distance. "Rest in peace," he whispered as the last glow vanished from sight.

Blood Magic

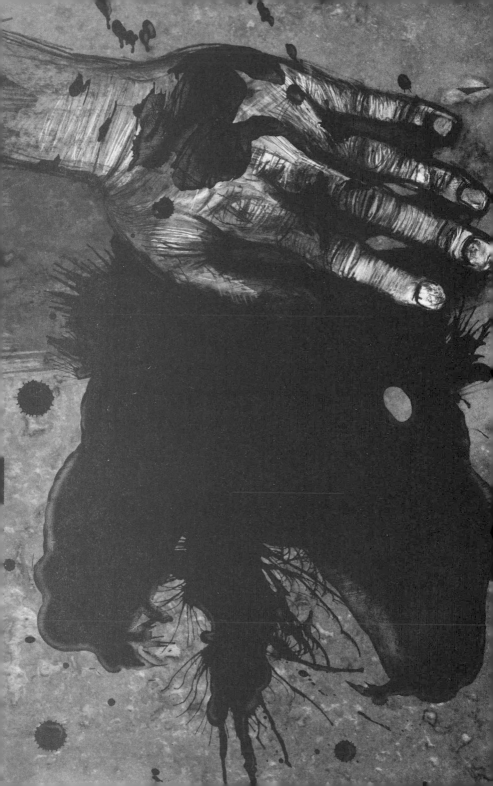

My downfall was a candy bar. Eddy Hilbert had a saltier craving. It was just the two of us in the store, just us and the night clerk. I'd been sitting at home, watching some stupid movie after my parents went to bed, when I'd gotten a craving. The store was only two blocks away.

Eddy came in after me. The clerk didn't pay much attention to either of us. I nodded toward Eddy. He nodded back. I didn't really know him. He was one of those kids in school who are sort of transparent. I'd see him in the cafeteria, or pass him in the halls. I couldn't even remember who he hung out with. Maybe he hung by himself. But we had a common bond. Both of us were about to pay a high price for our desires.

As I took my candy bar to the register, I saw Eddy heading for the chips. I guessed sour cream and onion, but he went for salt and vinegar. Live and learn.

I was reaching for my money when they came in. Two guys, walking fast. No mistake what they were after. Two guys wearing ski masks. One guy clutched a pistol; the other carried a shotgun.

Crap.

I froze. It was definitely not hero time. Not if I wanted to make it past the age of fourteen. *Be cool,* I told myself. I glanced toward Eddy. He'd frozen, too. Right at the end of the aisle. Smart boy. I'd never, ever been close to anything like this. Once, a kid in the boys' room at school had flashed around a hunting knife, trying to look dangerous, but he hadn't scared anyone. This was different. These guys had the power to hurt me. But just because someone has a power doesn't mean he'll use it. With luck, they'd clean the register and get out fast.

The guy with the shotgun stood back, covering me and Eddy. The other guy pointed his pistol at the clerk and said, "Now!"

The clerk opened the register with shaky hands and started stuffing money into a bag. But he got this strange look on his face. *Don't do it,* I thought, praying that I was wrong. But as he lifted the bag with his right hand, his left hand went under the counter.

I flinched, expecting him to come up with a gun. But he didn't. Instead, he fumbled underneath the counter for a second like he was feeling around for something. I had no idea what he was doing.

But the guy with the shotgun did. "He hit the alarm. Let's get out of here."

It's almost over, I thought. They'd leave now. The edges of my terror eased as I realized I wasn't going to die.

The guy with the handgun didn't listen to his buddy. He swore at the clerk, then pulled the trigger.

My guess is the pistol was a .22. It didn't make much of a pop. Barely more than a hand clap. But it was enough. The clerk straightened up like he'd gotten a jolt of electricity through his body, then dropped to the floor.

"Stu!" the other guy said. "Oh, man—now we're fried. Come on, the cops gotta be coming."

"No names, you idiot!" Stu shouted. He turned toward me, raised his gun, and pointed it at my face. He kept looking from me to the counter and then back, as if trying to decide whether one murder was any more of a problem than two. The sight of the open muzzle brought my fears to new heights. I wondered whether to duck and run, or try to dive at him and grab the gun. Whatever I did, there wouldn't be any second chances.

"Don't try anything!" Stu told me. "You're coming with us. Both of you." He waved the gun away from my head, toward the door.

"You crazy?" the other guy said. "They're just kids."

"Hostages," Stu said. "The cops can't hurt us if we got hostages." He aimed the gun back at me. *"Move it!"*

I moved it. They herded us toward a van, then pushed us in the side door. There were no seats in the back. I sat on the floor. Stu got in the passenger side. The guy with the shotgun slid behind the wheel.

My heart felt like it would explode at any minute. Sweat rolled down my back, pasting my shirt to my skin. Next to me, Eddy seemed strangely calm, like he had everything under control. He whispered something, but I didn't catch it.

"Easy," Stu said as the van peeled out of the parking lot. "You don't want to get us pulled over."

We shot down the road. I noticed a key chain dangling from the ignition. White plastic with black letters. MIKE'S KEYS.

I looked up. Stu was watching me. He knew what I'd seen.

A moment later, I heard sirens far behind us. Hope flared, then died. The sirens didn't come our way. They were going to the store. More sirens wailed from ahead, rising in pitch.

"Stay calm," Stu said. "The cops don't know it's us."

"*Me* stay calm?" Mike said. "*You* popped that guy. Why'd you do it?"

"Doesn't really matter now, does it?" Stu said. Then he did something that pushed my fear back to the edge again. He took off his ski mask. "Damn thing's too hot," he said. "Take yours off, Mike. Don't want the cops seeing it."

The van swerved briefly as Mike took one hand from the wheel and pulled off his mask.

I looked away, but it was too late. I'd seen their faces. The sirens blared past us, rushing toward the scene of the crime. Blue and red flashes reflected off the windows and then vanished.

Odds were, I was dead. I knew their names. I knew their faces. Stu had already killed one person. There was nothing to keep him from killing two more. As soon as he no longer needed hostages, we were dead.

That was when Eddy decided to break his silence. "Hey, you freakin' moron, let us go."

I hadn't believed things could get worse. What was Eddy thinking?

He crawled forward and put a hand on the back of Stu's seat. "Come on, let us go."

"You want some of this?" Stu said, pressing the barrel of the gun against Eddy's forehead.

Eddy backed off. I had no idea what he was trying to do. He whispered something again. *My blood?* Was that what he was trying to say? There'd already been enough blood spilled. I didn't want to add mine to the pool.

"Stu, they've seen us with our masks off," Mike said.

"Yeah, I know." Stu raised the gun again. He looked like he was trying to make a decision.

I stared down at the floor. "I didn't see anything."

The van swung through a sharp curve. For a moment, I leaned against the door to keep from falling over. Then we straightened out. My hand rested against the door handle.

"Don't try it," Stu said.

Would he shoot me if I rolled out the door? It probably wouldn't matter. Not once I hit the road. I let my hand drop. My mind raced through a thousand blind alleys, looking for a way to stay alive. I saw one chance. "Hey, you shoot us, that's premeditated," I said. I didn't know a lot about the law, but maybe this would make a difference to him.

"No, I shoot you, that's pretty messy," Stu said. He laughed. The sound made my skin tingle.

"Then do it," Eddy said. He held up his hand. "Come on. You like it so much. Do it piece by piece." He thrust his hand out, fingers spread, palm facing Stu.

Two killers and a crazy hostage. Even my nightmares weren't this bad. I braced myself, expecting that the crack of a .22 would be a lot louder inside the van than it had been in the convenience store.

Stu aimed the gun lower. "How about a kneecap? Should I start there? Would you like that?"

My own guts twitched at the thought of a kneecap exploding. I figured Eddy would stop. But he wiggled his fingers. "What's the matter, Stu? Too hard a target? Here, let me move it closer for you." He pushed his hand toward Stu, like a cop stopping traffic.

Stu made this face. I'd seen it before. It was the face of a parent who's gotten tired of his kid asking for something over and over and has decided to give it to him just to shut him up.

The gun wasn't that much louder inside the van.

I saw Eddy's hand jerk. A little spray of blood shot out

the back. The bullet smacked the rear door, cratering the metal. The whole thing seemed so unreal, I just stared. And fought the urge to throw up.

"Happy?" Stu asked.

I would have been rolling on the ground, clutching my hand. Maybe screaming. I play guitar. I'm real careful about my hands. But Eddy hardly flinched. He just held his hand palm up, about six inches from the floor of the van, and watched it bleed.

Stu turned back to Mike. "We're cool. They aren't following us. Nobody made the van. We don't need hostages anymore."

"Where?" Mike asked.

"Let's take 'em down by the river."

I thought about diving for the steering wheel. The road was lined with trees. Maybe I could yank the wheel hard enough to crash us. They weren't wearing seat belts. Neither was I, but at least I'd know it was coming. Still, if I was leaning over far enough to grab the wheel, I didn't see how I could keep from flying through the windshield.

Even if I could get away, what about Eddy? He was mumbling something and moving his hand in a pattern above the floor of the van, watching his own blood drip. At first, I thought he might be leaving a clue for whoever investigated our murder. But it didn't look like he was writing words. All I could make out was a flattened circle and a couple of lines.

"Take a left up ahead," Stu said.

"I know where the river is," Mike said.

I recognized the top of the old train trestle out the side window. We were on Mill Road. The next left would take us down near the boat launch. There wasn't much time left.

"Eddy," I whispered, hoping he could help me jump them, or at least distract them. Maybe he could fling his hand and get blood in their eyes. Anybody would flinch if he was sprayed with blood. Even a killer.

Eddy ignored me. I called his name again. He just kept mumbling. I tried to figure out what he was saying, but the words made no sense. They didn't even sound like English.

I braced against the side of the van as we turned left. A moment later, we turned again. A sharper turn this time, cutting back to the right. I could hear the surface beneath the tires change to gravel. We were on the access road to the river. There wouldn't be any traffic. Nobody comes here since they built the new boat launch up by Twin Forks.

If I was going to dive for the wheel, it had to be now. I looked at Eddy again, wondering whether I should warn him to hang on.

The van stopped.

"End of the line," Stu said. He pointed the gun at me. "Let's move nice and slowly."

I heard my own heart beat. Then I heard a different sound.

Something hissed like boiling water.

The hiss bubbled up from the floor of the van. The blood—Eddy's blood—began to move. It slid together, growing thicker. One end of the circle formed into a blob the size of a baby's fist.

"Come on," Stu said. "Let's get this over with."

I glanced up at him. He hadn't noticed what was happening. I looked at Eddy. He winked at me and whispered, "Blood magic."

The blob was now a head, shaped like a lizard but covered with red feathers. The head was mostly mouth.

The mouth was mostly teeth. Behind the head, a body took shape—long, slinky like a ferret, supported by short legs with claws. All red. Bloodred.

Something cold pressed against my cheek. The hard edge of the .22 dug into my skin. "Let's go!" Stu said. "Don't make me ask again. Not unless you love pain as much as your friend does."

Eddy raised his bloody fist and shouted a word that made no sense to me.

The blood beast leaped at Stu. It tore into his throat. His arms shot up. A crack, far louder than the others, deafened my right ear as the gun fired inches from my head. The bullet tore through the roof of the van.

Stu let out a gurgling scream. Then a whimper. Then nothing. The creature seemed to be slowly dissolving in the bath of blood.

Mike, wide eyed, had watched all this, as paralyzed as I was. Finally, grunting an incoherent scream of his own, he reached for the shotgun. Too late. The blood creature, its rear legs now half dissolved, jumped the short distance from the passenger seat and landed on Mike's face with the splat of a wet washcloth.

I turned away. Mike's scream grew louder, rising in pitch. It stopped as quickly as Stu's. I didn't want to look at him.

Something splashed to the floor next to me. It was barely recognizable now. Half the body had dissolved. The front claws swiped feebly at the air. In seconds, the creature melted into the growing pool of Mike and Stu's blood.

Eddy was drawing again, dipping his finger in the small puddle of his own blood, then sketching more designs on a clean area of the van's floor.

As I stared at him, he glanced up. "Sorry," he said.

"What?"

"Same problem they had." He motioned with his head toward the front of the van. "You've seen behind my mask. You're a witness." He turned his attention away from me and continued his blood magic.

The new creature formed quickly. A head—this time like a snake—rose from the floor. Eddy added two short legs to the front of the body.

I scuttled away. My fingers bumped into something that slid from contact. I groped for the gun. "Stop it." I raised the .22 and pointed it at Eddy.

He didn't look up. Beneath the snake head, narrow shoulders lifted from the diagram of blood.

"I'll shoot." As I spoke, my hand trembled. The first jolt was so strong, I almost pulled the trigger by accident.

"No, you won't," Eddy said. "You aren't the cold-blooded kind."

"And you?"

"This blood is far from cold," Eddy said. He stared at me with the same expression I'd seen when Stu was deciding whether to kill us. Then Eddy smiled. He stopped moving his hand. The beast, already trying to crawl with its forelegs, remained unfinished.

"On the other hand . . ." He paused and smirked as he looked at his wounded hand and then his drawing hand. He wiggled the bloodstained tip of his index finger at me. "On the other hand, no one would believe you if you talked," Eddy said.

"I'm not planning to talk."

"I could use a friend," Eddy said. "It would be nice. We could do stuff together. Hang out. Yeah, I'd like that. I could teach you all kinds of things." He held his right hand toward me. Blood dripped slowly to the floor of the van. "Let's shake on it."

I froze as my mind weighed the horror of being friends with him against the certain death that would come if I refused. It seemed as bad a choice as the one between the bullet and the road.

"Let's shake!" Eddy flung his hand out. A spray of droplets hit my face and I flinched.

That's when my fist clenched. I felt a jolt through my wrist as my hand kicked up in the air. At first, I wasn't even sure where the shot came from. Eddy opened his eyes wide. He looked at the gun in my hand. I looked at the gun. Then Eddy fell forward onto the pool of blood on the floor of the van.

I thought it was finished.

Then Eddy moved. I hadn't killed him. Relief flooded through me.

But it wasn't Eddy that was moving. It was something beneath him. Something red and solid began to emerge from under Eddy. The blood beast, its snake tongue flickering red in the air, tore itself free with a sound like a boot lifting out of mud. The front legs pulled the body from under the dead weight of Eddy. There were no back legs. The body of the beast ended where the transformation had stopped. The creature couldn't grow any further without Eddy's blood magic. But it could move. It crawled and slithered toward me.

I emptied the gun into it, squeezing the grip with both hands. The bullets passed through, leaving no mark. I yanked open the side door and tumbled from the van. Behind me, I heard a moist smack as the blood beast fell to the gravel.

I ran. It chased me, slithering, skittering, streaking across the ground. Only a lack of back legs kept it from catching me immediately. As it was, I barely managed to stay ahead.

Water. I ran toward the river. Blood and water. The beast would lose its shape. Dissolve. I ran down the bank and into the shallow water at the river's edge. The half-formed creature followed me. I ran through ankle-deep water, slipping on the algae-covered rocks. I looked over my shoulder and realized my mistake.

The blood beast shot through the water faster than it had moved on land, no longer hindered by a lack of rear legs. There was no sign that the river caused it any harm.

I fell. My hands clutched at the rocks and I tried to drag myself up.

The beast was nearly upon me.

Blood.

It dissolved in blood.

I hesitated for an instant as I thought about my guitar. A very brief instant. I slammed my palm against the corner of a rock. I felt a sharp sting, then numbness. I grabbed at the beast as it reached me, wrapping my fist around its neck, putting my bleeding palm against its bloodflesh.

If I was wrong, I was dead for sure.

I'd expected it to be slippery, but the skin was hot and firm. It tried to fling itself free of my grip. Its strength was almost more than I could handle.

But I could feel the body dissolving beneath my hand. I wrapped my other hand around my fist and squeezed harder, willing the blood to pump from my wound.

The creature hissed, angry, raging against my hold.

The neck dissolved. The ends parting. I opened my hand. The head fell into the water and rolled away with the current. The body twitched, then grew still. It lost its solidity, spilling into the water like hot candle wax.

I rinsed my hands in the river, staggered back to the shore, then dropped to my knees. I didn't try to fight the nausea this time. I just let my body purge whatever it could. My hand was still bleeding. I watched the blood trickle to the ground. For some reason, I moved my hand, drawing a figure on the flat surface of a rock—sketching a crude outline of an animal.

Come to life, my mind whispered. "Live," I said out loud.

I watched the shape, unsure whether I was looking for proof of the magic, or assurance that Eddy's power wasn't in my blood. Overhead, a cloud brushed the face of the moon. The dark swirls on the rock seemed to shift beneath the changing light.

I squeezed my fist and stood, afraid to go any further. Turning from the rock, I stumbled to the van. I could see Mike pressed against the driver's window. I walked around the back of the van, then went to the passenger side. I halfway expected to find Eddy sitting there, playing with all the blood, drawing new horrors. But he was just the way I'd left him.

"Sorry, Eddy," I said out loud. "I didn't mean it."

I headed toward the road, wanting to leave all this behind me. I wanted to go back to the life I'd known, a life of school and television and late-night snacks. Not a life where any cut or scrape could spill temptation from my wounds.

But with each step, the images flowed through my mind. And with each step, the blood flowed through my veins, whispering its secrets. Whispering its magic. Waiting.

A Cart Full of Junk

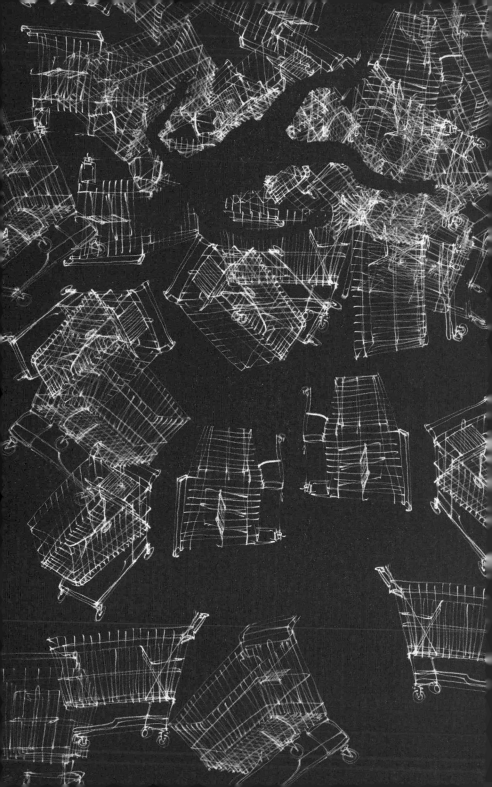

Turk was in a mood to do some harm. He was hanging out at the corner of Fourth Street, where the movies used to be. The place was boarded and shut, like almost everything else on the block. Gray was with him, along with Mackler, Johnny, and a couple of others. Across the street, an old guy came around the corner, pushing a shopping cart stuffed with junk. Bad timing.

Turk stepped away from the wall. "Let's go shopping."

He strolled across the street, angling to end up ahead of the old man. Gray and the others followed. There was no need to rush. The old guy couldn't run with the cart, and Turk knew there was no way he'd leave it behind.

The one flickering streetlight behind Turk jabbed his shadow at the old man like a spear. The rest of the lights had been shot out long ago.

"Hey, man," Turk said as the old man got close. "Mind if I look?"

The old man stopped walking but didn't speak. As Turk stepped toward the side of the cart, the old man reached under the blanket that draped the shapeless mound of possessions. Turk froze, ready to dodge if the guy pulled a knife. He'd seen street people could go crazy without warning, slashing out with a surprising fierceness. Turk knew how easy it was to end up sprawled across the curb in a puddle of blood and intestines.

The man removed something soft and small from beneath the blanket.

"A gift." As he rasped the words in a low voice, he flicked his arm. "From all of us."

"Hey!" Johnny shouted.

Turk turned and looked. Johnny was clutching whatever the man had thrown.

"Gloves?" Johnny held them up. "This is crap. There's a finger missing." He threw the gloves down.

Turk grabbed the edge of the cart. "You giving us junk?"

"Gifts," the man said. He barked out some sound between a laugh and a cough.

Turk shoved him with both hands. The guy had no more mass that a stack of paper bags. He tumbled, and stayed curled against the sidewalk. It was too easy to be much fun.

"Come on," Turk said. He led them away, in search of something more amusing. He found it soon enough.

Some fool had parked a new Altima on Third Street. Turk hadn't expected to stumble across such a generous gift that night, so he wasn't prepared to make the most of it, but he figured there'd at least be time to snatch the stereo and a couple of tires. Like a pit crew, they went to work at their usual tasks. Turk yanked the stereo while Gray popped the trunk and pulled out the jack.

It went fine until Johnny grabbed the right rear tire. The car slipped off the jack. The rim slammed down on Johnny's hand.

They left the tires, but Turk kept the stereo under his jacket when they dropped Johnny off at the emergency room. There was no point waiting for him. It would be hours. And the screams were getting on Turk's nerves.

Gray kept babbling about it the rest of the night.

"It wasn't my fault.

"I didn't make it slip.

"Johnny should have been more careful."

And on and on until Turk felt like hitting him in the face with a brick. It was as bad as the screaming.

The next night, Turk saw the old man again. As Turk

crossed the street, the man was already reaching into his cart. He pulled something out and threw it toward the group.

Gray caught it. "One sneaker? This is useless." He hurled it at the old man, nailing him in the shoulder.

"Yeah," Turk said. "What's wrong with you? You think we want junk." He pushed the old man down. Then he grinned. It might not be any fun to push the guy once, but it could become an enjoyable part of his nightly routine. He gave the guy a kick in the ribs, but not too hard. He didn't want to break him just yet.

"Let's go get Johnny."

When Johnny came to the door, his hand was wrapped in a huge wad of bandages.

"Freakin' mummy," Turk said.

"I lost a finger," Johnny told them.

Turk's gut rippled. He didn't like the idea of losing body parts. "You coming?" he asked.

"Yeah." Johnny joined them.

They walked ten blocks to the closest subway stop. Turk hoped there'd be something interesting underground. Something to play with. Or someone. But nothing exciting was happening.

Until Gray slipped on a piece of a meatball sandwich someone had dropped near the edge of the platform.

He fell at a bad time. There was an express train coming. He almost managed to scramble clear, but he got clipped. His left foot was mangled so badly, even Turk didn't have the stomach to look at it. At least Gray passed out, so they didn't have to listen to any screams as they carried him up the steps.

"One foot," Turk said aloud after they dropped Gray at the hospital. "One sneaker." He realized a person with one foot would need only one sneaker. And a person with a missing finger would need gloves with the same finger missing.

"Let's find that old man," he said. It was time to stop this. Whatever was happening, Turk knew how to end it.

They didn't find him that night. When Turk spotted him the next evening, two blocks from the subway, a chill ran through him. But he didn't back off. Fear was a sign of weakness. Weakness got you killed.

"Hey, you!" He jogged toward the old man. Turk expected him to keep walking, or to turn and run.

The old man did the unexpected. He shoved the cart toward Turk. Then he scurried for the corner. Turk didn't bother to chase him. He knew he could catch up with the guy after he checked out the cart.

"What's this crap?" Mackler asked, pulling aside the blanket.

The cart was filled with scraps of cloth. As far as Turk could tell, they were all the same. Turk reached in and lifted out a piece of knitted wool. The others all reached in and grabbed one. The shape seemed familiar, but incomplete. Turk noticed a label. SIZE 7½.

A hat? Turk thought.

"Half a hat," Mackler said, completing his thought.

Turk looked up. The old man was gone. He looked back in the cart just as Mackler pushed aside the mutilated hats, revealing an object underneath—something made of wires, batteries, a mousetrap, and several dark sticks the size of road flares.

Snap.

Turk's brain screamed for him to turn away, but the bright flash erupted too quickly for his body to obey. The explosive force struck him and the others full in the face.

When the rain of flesh and bone was finished, any of

the singed and smoking half hats scattered across the sidewalk would have fit nicely on what was left of Turk's head. Though Turk and his gang were beyond caring what they wore or how they looked.

Around the corner, the old man hadn't flinched at the sound of the explosion. He had other things on his mind. It was time to look for a new cart.

Morph

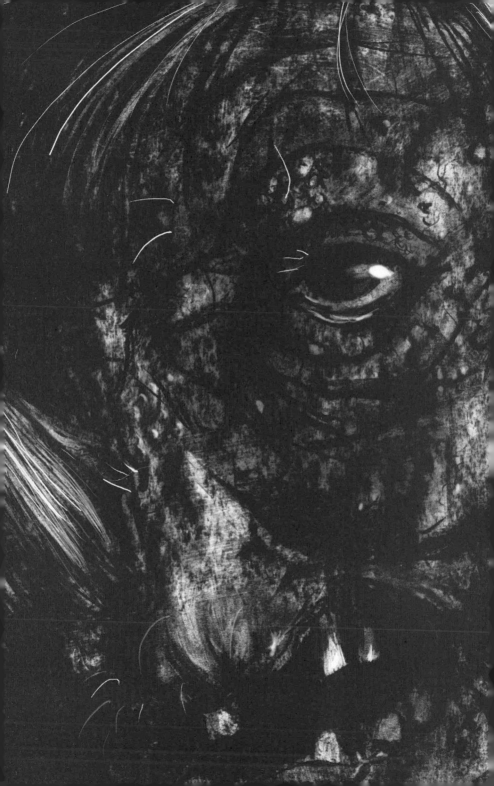

To a white boy like me, Chinatown is a movie, an adventure, and a horror show all rolled into one. To my friend John Fong, it's just home. No matter how often I go there to hang out with him, I'm always amazed by the activity. Everyone is moving, walking, talking, selling, and buying. The whole place seems to vibrate. I've heard there are bigger Chinatowns in other cities. Maybe so. But I'd bet there isn't a busier one.

John's parents own a bakery right around the corner from their apartment. It's not the kind of stuff I'm used to—not like the pastries they sell across the river or the fancy breads you can get uptown—but it's pretty good, especially since everything tastes better when you get it for free. John and I had just stopped by the bakery for a snack, and then headed to the Lucky Pleasure Arcade. We were on our first day of spring break from Jefferson High, so we were pretty much ready for some serious fun.

As we squeezed through the crowded streets, I scanned the food shops. You never knew what you'd see hanging from a hook or heaped up in a crate.

"Hey, Andy, check out the baby eels," John said, pointing to the window of a grocery store.

"Whoa, you eat those things?" I leaned over and watched the wriggling black strips in their water-filled pan. They reminded me of living rubber bands.

John shook his head. "My parents might. Not me. Too slithery."

A flurry of motion in a high-sided enamel tray to the left of the eels caught my eye. My subconscious survival instinct must have taken over, because by the time I realized what was there, I'd already jerked my face away from the window.

"Whoa!" I took a step back and pointed.

"Man, that's creepy." John leaned closer, so his forehead was pressed against the window. "I don't think my parents would eat one of those. Maybe my grandfather."

Still keeping my distance from the window, I stared at the panful of scorpions as they crawled over one another, forming a mass like one living creature with hundreds of claws and stinging tails. "Would you?" I asked.

"Not for a million dollars. But you got to admit you white boys eat some pretty disgusting things, too."

"Like what?"

"Like rare steak," John said. "It makes me think of those medical shows on TV. You slice through a slab of quivering meat with the knife, and the blood leaks out all over the plate. Nurse! Hand me the steak sauce! Hurry—he's bleeding out! Disgusting. And what about tuna salad?" He jammed a finger down his throat and made gagging sounds. "Now, that's something no civilized person would eat."

"It's still better than eating it raw," I said.

"You idiot. That's Japanese, not Chinese. You are so culturally uninformed."

"Excuse me, you all look alike. What can I say?"

"Not much," John shot back, "considering you bear an uncanny resemblance to a peeled potato."

It was a good thing the people passing by weren't listening. They might have thought we were serious. No way. I'd been friends with John since he moved here back in fourth grade. That was seven years ago.

"Come on," John said. He reached into his pocket and pulled out a handful of quarters. "We'll settle this like real men—head to head at the arcade."

As I turned away from the grocery, another motion caught my eye. The storekeeper stepped up to the inside of the window, snatched an angry scorpion from the pan with a pair of wooden tongs, and dropped it into a small cardboard box—the kind they use for takeout food. He handed the box to a customer. That's where I got my second surprise. From what little I could see through the dirty glass, the man wasn't Chinese.

Why would anyone buy a scorpion? I waited for the man to walk out so I could get a clearer look.

"Come on, Andy, let's get going," John said.

"Just a second." I had to see what he looked like. Maybe I'd even ask him why he'd bought it. Ever since I was little, I've been curious about stuff. I guess that's a nice way to say "nosy." Dad used to joke that I'd either end up as a scientist or a spy. Mom hammered me all through my early years with that saying about curiosity killing the cat. I'm pretty sure she's told me, "It's not polite to stare," at least seven thousand times.

It would be seven thousand one if she were here on the sidewalk right now. I couldn't help staring at the man when he stepped from the store—not because of what he'd bought, but because of what he lacked. His skin was as white as the carton he carried. So was his hair, which he wore long and parted in the middle. His eyes were pink. I'd seen albino animals before, but never a person.

He stared back at me. I was too transfixed by the layers of strangeness to look away. Then he lifted the box and shook it in my face. The scorpion rattled against the cardboard.

That broke the spell. I jumped aside.

He laughed and moved past me. After a few paces, he looked back over his shoulder, shook the box again, and smiled, revealing yellowed teeth. Then he slithered into the crowd.

"That was pretty much the strangest thing I expect to see this week," John said. "It's going to be hard for me to think of you as a white boy after this."

"You think he'll eat it?" I shuddered at the thought of him popping the living scorpion in his mouth and crunching it up like a piece of peanut brittle.

John shrugged. "Who knows?"

"What else would he do with it? I mean, he just bought one, so I think it's safe to say he isn't having the gang over for a scorpion fry."

"Maybe some kind of medicine," John said. "People

use all kinds of strange stuff—snake venom, animal claws, just about anything. When my aunt's shoulder hurts, she rubs this brown liquid on it. She keep the stuff in a jar with a couple of huge beetles and all kinds of roots."

"That's really weird," I said.

"So is using mold to kill bacteria," John said. "Or tree bark to cure a headache."

"Okay—you've got a point. But at least molds and trees don't feel pain. I'm not all that worried about bee-tles, either. But I heard they're wiping out the rhino just for the horn."

"It's supposed to be an aphrodisiac," John said.

"You mean an *Asian-disiac,*" I said, trying to make a joke.

John groaned. "Anyhow, that's what they use it for. They swear it helps them get horny."

It was my turn to groan. "How appropriate." As we walked toward the arcade, I thought about the sad state of a world where people would kill a rhinoceros just for the horn. My deep thoughts lasted less than a block and a half. Once we reached the arcade, my whole mind and body were centered on kicking John's butt at *Shock Fighter Deluxe.* Unfortunately, John was pretty centered, too. So, as usual, my fighter ended up on the ground while various parts of his body flew in separate paths through the air, leaving crimson trails of veins like dozens of scarlet tadpoles.

"Again?" John asked, grinning at me while the CONTINUE? timer counted down and his player tap-danced a victory celebration on the scattered remains of my inept warrior's innards.

"Nah, I'd better get home. If I'm late for dinner, Dad will make what we just did look like a pillow fight."

"Later," John said, moving off toward the pinball machines.

I left the arcade and cut through an alley toward the bus stop on Third Street. That's when I saw the albino again, just ahead of me. Halfway down the alley, he ducked into a narrow pathway between two buildings. I walked up to the opening and peeked around the wall. The albino was standing by a solid steel door at the end of the path, about fifteen feet away from me. It looked like the back entrance to some sort of business. He opened the carton and reached inside. The scorpion wriggled and slashed as it hung between his right thumb and forefinger.

He dropped the carton, then put the scorpion on his left palm. He stroked it gently with the tips of his first two fingers. I expected it to make a dash for freedom, or plunge its stinger into his palm, but it sat where he'd placed it, unmoving.

I watched, as frozen as the scorpion.

For a moment, what I saw was so strange, I didn't realize I was seeing anything at all. The images passed through my eyes and entered my brain. But they hung there like abstract forms—shapes with no meaning. His left hand changed. Somehow, it curved and shrank and drew toward his sleeve. The scorpion on his palm withered and shriveled like a leaf on an unwatered houseplant.

There was something beyond strange here, something unnatural and evil.

He raised his right hand and knocked at the door.

A minute passed. As much as I was dying to know what this was about, I found myself hoping nobody would answer.

I heard the clack of a bolt sliding open.

Whoever came out would see me. I stepped back into the alley, then squatted down so I could peek around the wall.

A middle-aged Chinese man wearing an expensive light gray suit stood in the doorway. He spat out a couple of words. I had no idea what he was saying, but he sounded angry.

The albino spoke, also in Chinese. Once or twice he touched the other man with his right hand. He seemed to be trying to calm him down.

The Chinese man spoke again. His face softened a bit and he stepped out from the doorway. He smiled and nodded.

The albino slipped closer and put his left arm on the other man's shoulder. His hand was still hidden within his sleeve.

I realized I was holding my breath. I exhaled, then inhaled quickly, gasping. To me, the sound was as loud as a shout, but neither of them looked my way.

A pale shaft emerged from the albino's sleeve. It slid into the other man's neck like a pump needle into a football.

For an instant, the victim didn't seem to notice he'd been stabbed. Then his mouth opened as if he wanted to shout. His hands rose toward his neck.

They never got there. His body jerked like he'd grabbed a frayed power cord. His eyes rolled back. His knees buckled. A sigh drifted from his slackening jaw. He would have fallen, had he not been pinned to that dagger. The killer finally lowered his arm, and his victim slid free, dropping to the street. His head bounced once against the pavement, the thud echoing between the buildings like an exclamation point.

I had no doubt he was dead.

As the albino turned away from the corpse, I ran out of the alley. People stared at me as I rushed away from Chinatown. The crowds actually parted as I passed among them. I must have stunk with fear. I felt I was leaving a trail.

I kept checking over my shoulder, but I didn't see the albino. He probably never knew I'd watched him.

Or maybe he didn't care.

The rest of the day seemed to take place at a distance. I know I ate dinner and went to bed, but part of me never left that alley. My first thought when I woke up was that I'd had some sort of vivid dream.

Unfortunately, I couldn't explain away my experience that easily. The murder made the paper. Next to last page. But nobody knew it was a murder. The article merely said that Shaoming Li, owner of the Golden Dragon Novelty Supply Company, was found dead of an apparent heart attack. The body was discovered by an employee.

I called John. "We gotta talk."

"It's not even noon. Can't it wait?" He sounded like he was still half-asleep.

"No. It's important."

"Okay. I'm awake now. Thanks to you. Come on over."

I thought about the alleys and the scorpions. "How about you come here?"

There was a pause. Then a click. He'd hung up. But that was okay. I knew he was on his way over. That's the kind of friend he was.

When John got to my place, I showed him the paper. "Did you know this guy?"

"Sure. Everybody knew Li. He's one of the three main

import-export guys." John winked, then said, "Import-export," again, as if it was a secret code.

The wink told me nothing. "I don't have a clue what you mean."

"Anything you want to bring into the country, Li was the man to see. Tiger paws, bear gall bladders, ivory—you name it. He was deep into all kinds of traffic."

"How do you know?"

"People talk. And they never pay any attention to me. They act like I'm just a kid. I hear stuff. But it's no secret. It's the same all over. Any part of the city, you'll find a couple of guys doing import-export. Chinese, Russian, Mexican, Irish. Crime is multicultural. I'm sure some of your Czech relatives or neighbors are involved in something."

"I'm not Czech. I'm Polish. And only half that."

"All you Slavs look alike to me," John said. "Anyhow, why this sudden interest? And what does any of this have to do with me getting robbed of sleep?"

"I saw something." That sounded like such an empty description.

"What?"

"You wouldn't believe me." I wasn't sure I really believed it myself.

"I might. Now that I'm awake. You got anyone better to tell?"

He was right. I told him. Sharing it, crazy as the whole thing had been, was a relief.

"You saw this for sure?" John asked after I finished the story. "You weren't that close, were you?"

"I was close enough." As I thought back, doubt invaded my memories. "It looked like a scorpion stinger. But maybe he just had something in his hand. I guess it could have been a long needle, or an ice pick. Or maybe some kind of knife."

"Forget it," John told me. "That's best. Just forget it. So what if he was killed? Do you think Li was some innocent businessman? I'm sure he had plenty of blood on his hands. Andy, these guys don't just import animal parts. They bring in guns. They bring in drugs. Maybe someone was just doing the world a favor."

I had no idea what I was supposed to do. I was the only one besides the killer who knew Shaoming Li's death was a murder. Normally, if you witness a murder, you have to speak out. It's the right thing to do. The tell us that in school. They tell us that in the movies and on TV. They tell us that in novels and comic books. But, right or wrong, there was no way anyone would believe me. I'm pretty sure John didn't. And there was no way I wanted the albino to learn that I was a witness. Maybe John was right. It was best for me to forget all about it. Or maybe I was just a coward, looking for an excuse. I decided it wouldn't hurt to think things over before I made a decision.

I was wrong.

The next murder happened two days later. Hop Ngo was found in the back of his restaurant. This death attracted a bit more attention than Shaoming Li's, though nobody knew it was a murder. Still, it was a vicious enough death that reporters swarmed all over the story. According to the paper, Hop Ngo had been attacked by his own dogs. The paper mentioned one strange item discovered at the scene. Along with a pair of live pit bulls, police found a third dog. But this one was a dried-up husk.

I was disturbed enough to track John down when he didn't answer his phone. His sister Katie, who was two years older than John, and two light-years better looking, let me in. I went to his room and held up the paper.

"There's been another killing."

John pulled the pillow over his face. "Are you going to wake me up every time someone from around here dies? Because if you are, I'm never going to get any sleep."

I yanked the pillow away and thrust the paper in his face. "Is this guy an importer?"

John sighed and took the paper from me. "Yeah. Hop Ngo was an importer. Different front operation, but he brought in the same kind of stuff as Li. They each had their own territory."

"It wasn't an accident," I said. "It wasn't his own dogs that killed him."

I could picture everything in my mind like it was a silent movie: It's late at night. The restaurant is closed, but Ngo is available for other business. The albino comes in. He brings a dog with him. Or maybe he grabs one of Hop Ngo's dogs. He presses the dog to his face and starts to change. His head becomes—

"Hey, Earth to Andy."

"Huh?" I realized John had been talking to me. "What?"

"Wow, you were drifting off toward elsewhere," John said. "Let it go. This has nothing to do with you. It doesn't even have anything to do with me. These guys live and die by their own rules."

"No. I can't let it go. This is about more than murder." I hated the thought of sharing my universe with a creature like that. "You said there were three importers. We have to warn the third guy."

"I'm sure he knows something's going on." John said, "Everyone in town is going to notice that two importers died."

"But he doesn't know about this creature. I have to warn him there's a killer stalking him."

"Sam Yung wouldn't listen to you," John said.

"Sam Yung," I said, repeating the name.

John groaned. "Man, forget the name. Please. He won't see you. You won't get near him. He's big trouble. He eats kids like us for snacks."

"I have to try." I walked out of John's bedroom. Behind me, I heard him running to catch up.

"Okay, just wait a sec while I throw on some clothes.

Maybe I can at least keep you from getting your throat slit while you try to find Sam. You're already pale enough."

"Thanks." I was glad he was coming.

We went into the depths of Chinatown to find the last of the big three importers. Unlike the other two, he didn't have one main front operation. I let John do the talking. We got yelled at a lot, and even spit at once. I didn't know if it was because we were asking about Sam Yung or because I was with John. But he was right—nobody takes kids seriously. Even kids old enough to drive and shave never get any respect.

We kept trying. If you knock on enough doors, eventually, you hear an answer. In the end, we didn't find Sam. It wasn't necessary. One of Sam's men found us.

This guy in a cheap brown suit, black shirt, and white tie slipped up from behind and tapped John on the shoulder. They talked in Chinese. Then John said, "Sam wants to know why we're looking for him. I told this guy that we had private business to discuss, concerning Sam's safety. He's taking us there. He said that if we annoy Sam, we'll end up tied to a couple of rocks at the bottom of the Naugus River. The fish will eat our eyes, and the turtles will dine on our tongues."

"Thanks for sharing that." I wondered how many different kinds of monsters I was dealing with. Maybe the ones who never shifted their shape were even worse than the unnatural killers.

It was too late to back out. We followed the guy down a maze of side streets toward an old, rickety building. There was no sign in any language out front—just a street number. We went inside, then climbed stairs that creaked beneath our weight. The banister was loose under my hand. I could swear I felt the building shifting under me. I smelled stale food on the first floor, but something darker and exotic took over as we moved past the second floor, up to the third.

"This whole place is falling down," I whispered to John.

The guy glared at me, hissed a couple of words at John, then led us down a hallway. It was too narrow to walk side by side. John went first. I was just a couple of steps behind him. We moved past several closed doors. There was an open door ahead on the right. John glanced in, then turned his head away like he'd accidentally looked straight at the sun.

I took a longer look. The room was large, but lit by a

single lamp on a table. That was enough for me to see more than I wanted. It was like someone had bombed a zoo. There were animal heads, paws, tails, skins, and other parts stacked all over. I saw a pile of elephant tusks, and another pile that looked like rhino horns. An old man at a table was grinding one of the horns into powder with a file. Except for the lamp, the scene could have been set five hundred years ago.

The guy with the cheap suit poked me in the shoulder and grunted out a couple of harsh syllables. I didn't know the words, but I'm sure it was the Chinese equivalent of *Get moving!*

We walked toward a door at the end of the hall. The upper half was frosted glass with S. YUNG, RESTAURANT SUPPLIES painted on it in black above a row of Chinese characters. Behind me, I could hear the rasp of the file on the rhino horn. But the sound was soon covered by the creak of the floorboards as they groaned beneath my weight. I was eager to get this over with as quickly as possible and return to the fresh air of the street.

The guy with the cheap suit opened the door and motioned us inside. He came in behind us, spoke a couple of words, then stepped out, leaving John and me alone with Sam Yung, the third importer. Sam was a thin guy in his forties, with the face of someone who's survived more than a couple of knife fights. The phrase "You should have seen the other guy" flitted through my mind.

"You are inquiring about me?" he asked as the door closed behind us. His English was better than mine.

For a moment, I couldn't find my voice. I knew this guy could snap his fingers and have me killed. I knew he was a criminal. But someone was planning to murder him, and I refused to keep quiet. "You're in danger," I said. My words died in the room like dialogue from a bad movie.

Sam Yung spread his hands. At least he didn't laugh at me like a villain from a bad movie. "It comes with the job. Half the punks in the city would kill me if they thought they could get away with it. What's the deal, here? I'm not going to find you amusing for very long."

"I saw what happened to Shaoming Li," I told him. "It wasn't his heart."

Sam Yung barely reacted, but I noticed a slight ripple of tension flash across his cheeks. "Tell me."

I told him what I'd seen happen to Shaoming Li, and what I suspected happened to Hop Ngo. When I mentioned the albino, Sam Yung nodded and muttered the name "Richter." When I was done, he said, "Has it occurred to you who would have the most to gain from the death of my competitors?"

Not until that instant. Oh, God. I'd never even thought that Sam Yung might be behind the murders. I felt like I'd just been kicked in the gut. I looked at John. He glanced over his shoulder, like he was thinking about making a dash for the door. But we both knew the other guy was right on the other side. I turned my attention back to Sam Yung.

The slightest smile twitched at his lips. "Foolish boy," he said. "That's not our way. We don't hire outsiders to solve our disputes. You know nothing about us."

I realized he was playing with me. "But you seem to know the man I saw. You called him Richter."

"I know of him. He's tried to benefit from my hard work. He wants what isn't his. But this other thing you spoke of, this is nothing but a children's story. My grandmother used to scare me with tales of shape-shifters. You have an active imagination. You're young. You don't know what you've seen. But I thank you for coming to warn me."

It didn't matter whether he believed me. All that mattered was I'd done what I had to do. I'd warned him. That might be enough. At least he wouldn't be easy to surprise, the way Shaoming Li had been. I was ready to leave.

But Sam Yung wasn't finished. He glanced at John, then back at me. "We have one problem that must be resolved. You've seen things you shouldn't have."

"We didn't see anything," John said. "Neither of us."

Now I understood why John had looked away from the room down the hall so quickly. There was enough illegal stuff going on in there to send Sam Yung to prison for a very long time.

"Of course I have your silence," Sam said to John. "You know what would happen to your family if you spoke." Then he pointed at me. "But I don't know if your friend can hold his tongue. Or whether it needs to be removed."

He stared at me with the cold eyes of a surgeon trying to decide whether to cut away a tumor.

I wanted to say something, but I had no idea what sort of words would make any difference to him. I knew it was useless to beg, or to point out that I'd gone out of my way to warn him. Maybe I could just swear I'd keep silent about what I'd seen. Before I could speak, the glass in the upper half of the door exploded. Something flew past me and thudded to the floor by Sam Yung's desk.

A head.

It took a moment for me to recognize the guy without his cheap suit. Or his body.

Someone—something—crouched outside the door. His face was all scales and teeth—somewhere between human and reptile. But it shifted back as I watched.

"Richter." Sam Yung snarled the name.

The albino reached into his coat pocket and drew out a furry brown claw. He held it to his body.

Across the room, I heard Sam Yung fumbling through a desk drawer.

I heard John whisper something in Chinese.

I heard the roar of a bear.

The albino crashed through the remaining portion of the door. His body was still rippling and changing. He dropped the dried claw on the floor. The lower half of his face was that of a bear. One hand was a claw. His massive shoulders stretched his shirt.

As he ran past us, he threw a backhanded swipe. The blow lifted me off my feet. John and I crashed into the wall.

For an instant, as my head and body struck the plaster, the room went soft and black. I fought the darkness, knowing that if I sank into the comfort of unconsciousness, I would never wake.

My head cleared just in time to see Sam raise a gun. His hand jerked as the gun spat out a small pop, no louder than a cap pistol. A patch of flesh in the albino's shoulder exploded in a mass of red.

It didn't slow him.

He crossed the room before Sam Yung could fire again. The claw swipe caught Sam under his chin. With no effort, the albino removed most of the man's face.

It happened so fast, Sam didn't seem to realize yet that he was dead. For a moment, as flesh and gore dripped down the splattered wall, and most of his jaw bounced across the floor like a shattered ashtray, he stood in place, a life-sized version of that plastic man in science class, half-exposed to the eyes of the curious, brain and muscle and bone revealed for all to see. A bubbling sound rose from the ruins of his throat. His tongue moved, as if searching for teeth.

Then he fell across his desk.

The albino turned toward us.

I staggered to my feet. "John, run!"

John didn't move. I reached down to help him up, but he was knocked out cold. There was no way I could carry him. There was no way I could protect him. There was nothing I could do for him except try to lure the monster away.

I ran into the hallway.

Heavy footsteps followed me.

Another of Yung's men rushed up the stairs. He pulled a gun from inside his jacket. It would be the final sick joke of my life if I ended up getting shot by the lesser of two evils while running from the albino. I ducked into an open doorway.

Outside, a single gunshot punched the air. Then I heard a scream overlapped by a wet, ripping sound. A body thudded down the stairs. I knew it was the gunman.

The albino stood at the edge of the doorway, red clots of skin dripping from his claw as it completed its transition back to a hand.

"My curious friend," he said, nodding toward me, speaking almost in a whisper. He pulled a handkerchief from his pants pocket and wiped his hand. "You have been a bit of an inconvenience. An amusing one, but an inconvenience nonetheless. I can't allow your continued existence."

I backed away from him. As the earthy stench of hides and bones hit my nostrils and I realized the full meaning of where I was, I lost hope. I'd truly screwed up. Of all the places to seek shelter, this was the worst imaginable.

"Lovely," the albino said, his eyes caressing the stacks of animal parts. He patted his coat pocket. "I brought my own supply, but this is truly splendid. What shall it be?"

He reached out to the nearest crate and stroked a wolf's head. "Our noble pal *Canis lupus,* perhaps?" His hand, where it met the gray fur, began to change. "I think not. Too swift. Wolves kill quickly, efficiently. They have no instinct for cruelty. You deserve better, my young friend." He studied me with those pink eyes. "I want you to linger. I want to savor our time together. Now, where would they keep the snakes?" He flicked his tongue like a serpent.

I moved deeper into the room. Beneath my feet, the wood creaked. Behind me, I heard a rasping breath.

The albino took another step. "Or maybe a leopard?" he said, reaching down to stroke a spotted skin. "Yes, that seems right. Cats play with their prey. Sometimes for hours. Thank goodness there's such a large stockpile. We're going to have so much fun."

I could hear the old man, the one with the file. He was crouched under a table, whimpering. I risked a glimpse over my shoulder. One chance . . . If I was wrong, I was dead. If I was right, I might still be dead. If I was right and very lucky, I'd live to have nightmares about today.

I plunged my hand into the box and scooped up a handful of the chalky powder. I threw it at the albino, trying to believe that this would save me. I threw a second handful, then a third.

He laughed. "Is that it? Your best effort? Oh my, I truly hope you give me more sport than that."

He reached to brush the dust from his cheek.

The change began.

For a moment, he seemed puzzled.

His hands grew thick. They grew large and gray, like dense lumps of clay. His face twisted and changed. His shirt split as his chest swelled. A horn thrust from where his nose had been.

He dropped to all fours with a heavy crash, then lowered his head, aiming the horn at me. He took a step with one hulking leg. And then another step. There was less than two yards between me and death.

A scream ripped through the room. But it didn't come from any living creature. The air filled with shrieks as the ancient wood gave way beneath the weight. One leg crashed through the floor. His chest hit with an ear-numbing boom.

For an instant, that was it. He raised his head toward me and bellowed a cry of rage. The eyes within the rhino's face were hot coals of hate.

He struggled to pull the leg free of the hole.

I backed up another step.

He fell.

He dropped so suddenly, it was almost as if he'd been sucked through the hole. An instant later, I heard another crash. Then another, fainter. And far away—a thud, a wet smack of flesh against concrete.

That was it. He was in the basement.

I inched toward the hole like I was moving on thin ice, expecting the floor to collapse at any moment. But the floor held. Down, far down—so far, I felt dizzy as I looked—lay a crumpled mass of white and red.

Around me, the lifeless eyes of countless animals

bore witness to the moment. A sound from down the hall caught my attention. I edged past the hole and went back to Sam Yung's office.

"How you doing?" I asked John.

He'd managed to sit up with his back against the wall, but still looked pretty dazed. "Did we win?" he asked.

"Yeah." I held out a hand and helped him to his feet.

He winced. "Oh, man. My head hurts."

"That's okay," I said. "You should see the other guy."

I walked with John back to his place. As we passed through the streets of Chinatown, I thought about how foreign each of us is when we leave our small part of the world, and how much there is that none of us will ever understand.

"You know what's scary?" I asked John when we reached his front door.

"Your face?"

"Besides that."

"I can't imagine anything scarier, but go ahead."

"If Richter was a bigger monster than Sam Yung, I guess it's possible there's someone out there who's a bigger monster than Richter."

John patted me on the shoulder. "If there is, I'm sure

you'll run into him. And drag me along. But maybe that
can wait for another day."

"Fine with me."

At least I knew there was a little less evil in the world.
It was a small change, but a good change. And that's
something to be glad about.

Whoodoo

You come in for a spell," the whoodoo lady said.

I nodded twice, once for each possible meaning. She swung open the door of her shack. I was relieved my knock hadn't broken it from its hinges.

"Don't be shy," she said.

I followed her in.

"I have whoodoo for finding gold," she said, pointing to a dried rabbit's head. "That one cost ten thousand dollars." She grinned, showing that the first gold I'd find would be in her mouth.

I shook my head. With what I was getting under the table rebuilding engines for the guy down the block, I'd need to work for years to raise that kind of money.

"Kill a man?" she asked, pointing to a tarry black root shaped vaguely like a person. "That be five hundred. Worth every penny. Never fail."

"Not today," I said.

"Five hundred is cheap to kill a man."

"Maybe some other time," I said. Even that would take me a month to earn.

"What about love?" she asked.

I nodded, and hoped it came cheaper.

The whoodoo lady let out a laugh. "A strapping boy like you. What he need with love spells?"

"It's for my father," I said.

"He not look like you?"

"A little. But that's not it. He's divorcing my mother. I figured, if he loved her again . . . well, you know . . ."

"I know, boy," she said. She moved to a corner of the room and picked up a dried flower. "Love is easy."

"How much?"

"Not five hundred," she said. "For sure. To kill is hard. To love is easy. Only fifty."

I gave her the money and took the flower. "How do I use it?" I imagined some intricate ceremony, possibly involving full moons, spilled blood, and candles.

"Crumble it over their shoes. Half on his. Half on hers."

"That's all?"

"Love is easy," she said again.

I left and did as she asked, crumbling the dead, dried petals and brushing the flakes on two pairs of shoes.

It worked immediately. Dad moved out of the basement. They went to dinner the next night, and to a movie the night after that. They went dancing three times the next week.

I came home one night less than a month later to find Mom sitting at the kitchen table, her face bruised. Like before.

"I fell," she said.

"Was it Dad?"

She shook her head.

"It was him, wasn't it."

"You don't understand," Mom said. "That's just his way. He doesn't mean to hurt me."

"But—"

"He loves me," she said. "More than ever. He loves me so much. So very much. He always will."

I got up from the table and headed for the door.

"Where are you going?" Mom called.

"I need to see if I can pick up more hours at work," I said. Just for a while. Just until I had five hundred dollars.

The Ex Box

t's not a date, Vida told herself as she stepped into the grease-scented air of the Lamberton Diner. *It's just coffee.* No way she was dating so soon after ending her three-month mistake with that loser drummer whose name she would never ever mention again. She'd already exiled his vital statistics to *the box.* She wondered whether she'd need a larger container soon. The box was getting full.

"Over here," Art said, walking past the PLEASE WAIT TO BE SEATED sign.

Vida hesitated.

Art glanced back and said, "I got my own spot."

As she followed him down the narrow aisle between chrome counter stools and vinyl booths, she noticed the waitress nod at him. A fair assortment of the other diners exchanged greetings with him, too. Vida caught a couple of lingering glances as they checked out the newcomer. No big deal. She wasn't shy. Art stopped by a table near the end of the row and waited for her to slide in on one side.

"Coffee's good here," he said as he took a seat facing

her. "Great fries. Decent pie. Stay away from the chili unless you want to . . ." He made a face and let the sentence dangle unfinished.

"Pie sounds right," Vida said, pleased that he hadn't resorted to crudeness—unlike that mechanic she'd dated last year. This guy was gorgeous. She had a weakness for skinny guys with dark hair and dark moods. Too bad that nine out of ten of them turned out to be jerks. Or ten out of ten. She'd spotted Art at the party the moment she walked in. She could tell he'd spotted her, too. He was cool about it, but she'd felt a slight tingle run down her neck as she turned away, as if his eyes caressed her from afar. She'd waited. She wasn't chasing anyone. Not anymore.

Soon enough, he'd glided across the room, moving dark and silent as a storm cloud, and introduced himself. After a couple of minutes of small talk, during which Vida verified that he was interesting and possibly worth getting to know, she'd asked, "You in a band?"

"Don't play. Don't sing. I listen. Mostly to composers who've been dead for two or three hundred years." He gave her a nostalgic smile. "Those were the days."

"Great." She'd had her fill of musicians.

They'd stayed together for the rest of the party, during which she discovered, much to her relief, that he had no interest in monster trucks, *Star Trek,* existentialism, or any of the other annoying obsessions of her last string of guys. If she never had to visit another racetrack, it would suit her just fine. As they left the party, heading loosely together toward the door, he'd suggested the diner.

Vita had agreed. *It's not a date,* she told herself as she followed him in her car.

When the waitress came by, Vida noticed that Art waited for her to order first. Nice. It blew her away how most guys didn't give any thought to the small touches.

"Coffee," she said. "And apple pie."

Art nodded, as if he approved of her choice.

"Ice cream?" the waitress asked.

"No, thanks." She'd gone through a half gallon in the week after the split. That was part of the ritual, too. Rip the name and address of the moron from her memo book, stuff it away in the Band-Aid box, then stuff her face until the chill killed as much feeling as possible.

"The usual?" the waitress asked Art.

"Sure, Gretta," Art said.

Gretta tucked her order pad in her apron and walked off.

Art checked his watch.

"Curfew?" Vida asked. She didn't even know if he lived at home. He looked like he was around nineteen.

"I have to be somewhere at three," he said. "What about you?"

"Two," she said. Her folks were pretty good about that, now that she was a senior. Even last year, they'd let her stay out until midnight on the weekends. She'd repaid the trust by keeping her grades up and not doing anything so stupid that it would permanently destroy her future. There'd been a couple of close calls, but no disasters. She glanced at her own watch. It was only twelve thirty. They had over an hour.

Gretta returned with two thick white mugs of black coffee. Vida reached for the Sweet'N Low. Penance for the ice cream would be a lengthy affair. Across the table, Art picked up the saltshaker, tilted it over his mug, and tapped the side twice.

"Acquired taste," he said in response to her unasked question.

"Hey, I used to dip potato chips in mustard," Vida

said. If this was as weird as Art got, she'd be thrilled. He had looks, he had manners, and he really did listen to her. She had a feeling he'd let her talk all night if that's what she wanted. The only time Art took his eyes away from hers was when he looked at his watch. Or when he tapped a bit more salt into his coffee.

Vida found she was glancing at her watch, too. She wanted the evening to last longer. But if it was meant to be, they'd meet again.

"I guess I'd better get going," she said as curfew drew close. She reached for her wallet.

"I've got it," Art said.

"Thanks." Vida stood, wondering whether to give Art a friendly hug. Guys were so good at misjudging things. One brief squeeze and they wanted to drag you off to their cave.

"I'll walk you out," he said.

As she pulled her car keys from her purse, Art touched her shoulder so lightly, she could barely feel his fingers. "I'm glad we met."

"Me, too."

They exchanged phone numbers. *Let's hope this one stays out of the box,* Vida thought.

She slept well. From the time she drifted lazily awake late the next morning to the time the sun set, she waited for the phone to ring.

"Call him?" she said aloud as she stared at the mute face of her cell phone. She didn't want to seem desperate—mostly because she wasn't desperate. But last night had been nice. More than nice.

He called at nine.

"Coffee?"

"Sure."

"Meet you there?"

"Sounds good."

The evening was as pleasant as she'd hoped.

"Are you around during the week?" she asked as they left the diner.

He shook his head. "I work pretty long hours."

Vida waited for him to give more details. Instead, he asked if he could take her to another party next Friday.

And so it went for a month. And then a second month. Vida met Art at the diner, or at a party. But he wouldn't tell her his address, or where he worked.

All she knew for sure was he went somewhere each evening at three.

It wasn't hard to follow him. She'd pleaded for a one-time curfew extension, and her parents had reluctantly agreed. When she left the diner, she circled the block, parked down the street, and waited for Art to go to his car. She let him get several blocks ahead, until the taillights had shrunk to the size of embers on a pair of dying candle wicks. Then she drove in his trail. Eventually, he pulled to the curb in the middle of a block of abandoned buildings and stepped through the door of a dilapidated movie theater. There were a dozen other cars along the street.

Vida watched as five more people went in after him. She recognized several of them from the diner. Finally, when there'd been no traffic for at least twenty minutes, she left her own car and walked quietly to the theater.

Do I want to do this? she thought as she pushed the door open. Unlike the old doors in horror movies, this one moved silently. Vida's own sigh of relief was louder.

She crept through the lobby. Quiet voices drifted from ahead. She moved to the inner door of the theater and opened it a crack.

"My name is Art."

She recognized his voice.

"Hi, Art," a roomful of other voices said, as if it was a ritual response.

Vida clutched the edge of the door as Art spoke. "I'm a vampire. I've been blood free for nearly eleven months."

"Good for you, Art," someone called.

The blood drained from Vida's own hands and face as she let go of the door and backed away.

She turned and fled, her steps echoing in the abandoned streets.

No. It has to be a joke. He was in some sort of pretend group. Like the people who wore armor and fought at festivals with wooden swords. Or the kids who dressed up like they were in a science fiction movie. This was play. Pretend. This was *Rocky Horror.* Dress up. Make-believe. This wasn't real. Not Art. Not her dear, sweet, gorgeous Art.

But her heart and soul knew otherwise.

When she got home, Vida ripped his number from her memo book, and grabbed the box. But she couldn't bring herself to cram the paper into the remaining narrow space.

He called the next evening, inviting her to coffee.

Vida went.

"I know," she said after they'd given Gretta their order.

"Know what?" he asked.

She stared at him without answering, unable to swallow. She could feel her pulse hammering at her throat.

"Sorry. That was beneath me." He spread his hands and glanced away, then looked back at her. "How'd you figure it out?"

"I followed you to your meeting," she said.

He sighed. "I'm doing pretty good. Another month, and I'll get my one-year pin."

"You should have told me," she said.

"I didn't think we'd go out more than once or twice. I haven't had much luck with relationships. I never thought I'd start to care for you. And then, I was afraid to lose you. I guess it's over. . . ."

Vida shook her head. "Darn it, Art. I think I love you."

"I love you, too."

She put her hand on his. "So. This meeting you go to, to keep from drinking blood. It works?"

"It's been working for me for thirty years."

She pulled her hand from his. "I thought you said you'd been going for almost a year."

"No. I've gone almost a year without a slip. Or a sip." He started to smile, but she locked her eyes on his.

"This is serious," Vida said. "What you're saying is you can't resist forever. Right?"

"Right."

"But after you slip, you can go a long time."

He nodded. "Right again."

"I guess I have no choice," Vida said. She reached for her purse.

"No choice. You should leave right now," Art said.

"And walk out on the best guy I've ever met? No way." Vida pulled the box from her purse and put it on the table.

"What's that?" Art asked.

"Names. Addresses. Think of it as a takeout menu."

Art slid the box from the table. "Old flames?"

Vida nodded. "They're a bit cold-blooded. But that can't be helped."

"Thanks. I'll be gentle," Art said as he tucked the box in his coat pocket.

"Please don't," Vida said. She picked up the saltshaker as Gretta placed a cup of coffee in front of her. "So it's good like this?" she asked.

Art shrugged. "I like it."

Vida gave the shaker a tap.

Art pulled out the slips of paper, then offered her the empty box. "Want it back?"

Vida took a sip of her coffee, then shook her head. "I won't be needing it." *Not bad,* she thought as she took a second sip. The coffee tasted different from what she was used to—a bit strange, a bit exotic—but she suspected she'd grow to like it, too.

Evil Twin

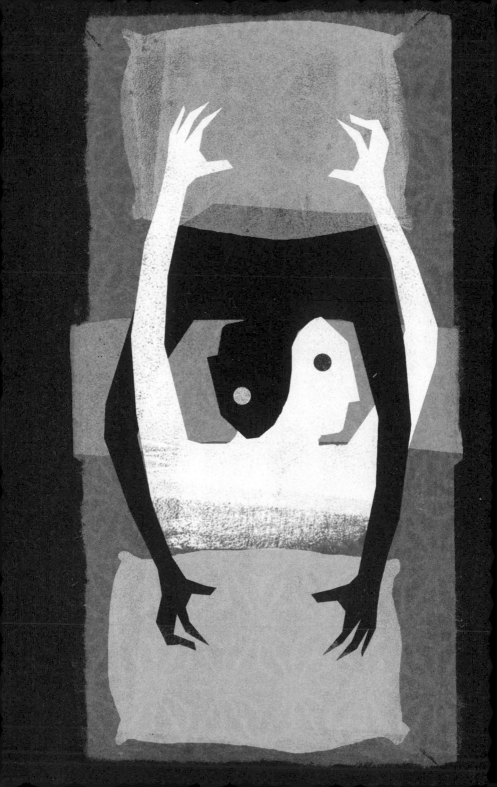

First, they said it would be the end of civilization. Then they said they were close to a cure. All of this scared me to death. All the kids were scared. We checked our fingers every day. We whispered the things we'd heard the adults say to each other when they thought we weren't listening.

It was an experiment that went wrong.

They made it in a lab.

It came here on a meteor.

One of my friends, Carly, spent so much time staring at her hands that our teachers had to take her out of class.

"Don't worry," Mom said every time I told her I was scared. "You won't catch it."

"Nothing is going to hurt my little girl," Dad said.

I tried to believe them. I tried not to worry. Then my thumb started to split. I noticed it right after lunch on a Monday three weeks before my eleventh birthday. I stared at the end of my thumb, unable to believe what I was seeing, but knowing in my heart that the thing I feared the most, the thing I *knew* would get me, had finally struck.

I started screaming. By the time my panicked mind finally tried to think of ways to hide my hand, it was too late. My screams had betrayed me. All the kids backed away from me. The teachers took me to the nurse's office and kept me there until the Health Squad came.

Now, I'm in the waiting place. I'm not sure which one. I guess it doesn't matter. They have them all over the world. Even though it isn't supposed to be contagious, they don't take any chances. I've been here a week, now. It's moving quickly. My arms and legs have both almost fully divided.

It doesn't hurt. I knew it wasn't supposed to. But there is more than one kind of pain. The pain you can feel in your flesh is nothing compared to the pain that rises from a horror you can't escape.

I'd heard that most victims pass out during the final days. That's good. Because the head is the last part of the body to split. I can't imagine what it will be like when I wake up. I have one chance in two that I'll be all right. Well, not really all right. I'll never be all right again.

I've had time to read. Even though I'm just a kid, the people here believe in explaining what is going on, and giving me books. They're overworked, and the place is too crowded, but the people try to be nice, even if they never look me in the eyes.

The scientists call it prion-induced microreplicant syndrome. Real people call it Jekyll–Hyde disease. My body is duplicating itself. I'm splitting into two people. Other than the indescribable horror of looking at my body and seeing two pairs of arms, the split itself might not be all that awful once it's finished—if the split just made an exact copy of me. But brain cells aren't like other cells. There will be two of me when this is over. Identical on the outside. But completely opposite on the inside. The scientists have big names for all of this, too. But, as always, the people have a simpler way to say things. After the split, there will be a good Samantha and a bad Samantha.

That was one of the things that became obvious as soon as the first Jekyll–Hyde victims awoke. The evil ones were clever enough to try to hide their nature, but they were so deeply and darkly evil, without any hint of good, that they couldn't disguise their darkness for long. They're kept away from the rest of society for the safety of everyone.

The good ones, on the other hand, were so nice and so trusting that they couldn't survive in the real world without help.

I've never been really bad. But I don't like the idea of being all good. And I hate the idea of being all bad.

There will be two of me soon. And I don't know which one I'll become. Maybe I'll be both. I don't know. The scientists have theories about what happens to your identity when you split. I really don't understand that part. It's confusing.

I've been getting more and more sleepy the last couple of days. The doctors explained that my body is working so hard to duplicate itself that it's using up a lot of energy. They have me hooked up to tubes. I'm on oxygen to help me breathe.

I really just want to sleep. I think I'll close my eyes for a while.

My mind feels much clearer. It's dark. I'm awake. There's still an oxygen mask on my face, but I don't think

I need it. My body feels normal again. The extra weight is gone. I look at my hand. Just one. The split is over.

I search my brain for evil impulses. Nothing. That's such a great relief. I look to my right. There's someone on the next bed. Me. How strange to look at myself. But it's the evil me. She isn't awake yet. I can't hear any sound from the nurses down the hall.

I get out of my bed. I take my pillow. Her life would be terrible. I know what I have to do. I remove her oxygen mask and put the pillow over her face. I lean against it. She struggles for a moment, but I am strong.

I smile, because I'm removing evil from the world. I am good. I have survived.

About the Author

David Lubar grew up in Morristown, New Jersey. His books include *Hidden Talents,* an ALA Best Book for Young Adults; *True Talents; Flip,* a VOYA Best Science Fiction, Fantasy, and Horror selection; the Weenies short-story collections *In the Land of the Lawn Weenies, Invasion of the Road Weenies, The Curse of the Campfire Weenies, The Battle of the Red Hot Pepper Weenies, Attack of the Vampire Weenies,* and *Beware the Ninja Weenies;* and the Nathan Abercrombie, Accidental Zombie series. He lives in Nazareth, Pennsylvania. You can visit him on the Web at www.davidlubar.com.